About the Author

Rabih Ballout is the owner
of multiple patents in the
technology field. He is
founder and CEO of various
companies, such as RadGio,
a radio-advertisement
platform for smartphone
users, and PayGeo, a mobile
cash-transmission system
utilizing ATMs and vending
machines. Ballout emigrated
to the United States in 1981
from Mt Lebanon and studied
mechanical engineering at
San Francisco State University.
An experienced entrepreneur
in nontechnology companies,
he has built, owned, and
designed display showcases
for the food industry. Ballout
is also an accomplished artist
in the traditional school of
oil painting. Some of his
works are featured in the
book. Although *Homo Electrus*
originated in his dreams, it
draws largely upon personal
experience and travels abroad

www.rabih.us

Introduction

As far back in my childhood as I can remember, and continuing to the present day, most of my dreams have consisted of reading old, ragged newspapers. The dreams were hardly predictable, and as much as I tried to play catch-up, going to bed in an attempt to continue where I had left off, I was not always successful. I would read through the pages describing past events, feasts, and headline stories, some historically factual and some not. It seemed as if I were transported to a different time zone. I would read and critique articles of the past and think either "They got it right this time" or "How sad that they did not know the truth."

I seldom remembered much of what I "read" in my dreams, but I seized on the rare occasions when I did. I would become obsessed with seeing if what I was reading had actually taken place, or if the names of places and people were real. Case in point: In a dream, I read a French newspaper article about a horrific mining disaster that took place in a little town called Courrières on March 10, 1906. I made a point to look at the date, as it was stuck in my head. I remembered the odd town name and decided to find out if the tragedy had really happened at that time. To my surprise, it had: 1,099 miners, including children, had lost their lives. I did not know what to make of it; the details were just too familiar. It was embarrassing to talk about, as a dream involving past events meant very little to people. Dreams of the future would be far more exciting. If I could tell what was forthcoming, now *that* would be interesting, especially if I got it right. Sadly, my gift seemed to be a reverse psychic power. Reading newspapers from the future would have to wait.

It seemed best that I go through my busy daily life without an added layer of pointless questions. All went well for a while, until my nightly dreams progressed in complexity and I began to remember them more during the day. Other nocturnal anomalies began to appear. One that I could never forget occurred during a real life visit to the town of Perugia in Italy. I had not planned a stop there but needed to drive through the area on my way to Pisa from Ancona on the Adriatic. Along the main highway, Perugia stood high above the cliffs with a striking view that drew my attention and made me exit the highway without much thought. I headed for the *citta vecchio* (old city), parked my car, and headed to the main piazza. There, a sweat came over me. Everything around me looked eerily familiar. I walked to the center of a place called Piazza Scotti, not far from an Etruscan well, and looked at the magnificent view below. I knew exactly where the baker shop lay, although it was now a restaurant. I looked to the north where the church of Saint Severo stood, exactly as I had predicted. I had no recollection of the names, but I knew the places; I felt that I had walked, lived, and breathed the air in that town and its surroundings. How could it be? I had been born hundreds of miles away, and I had never been in this part of the world, but here I was, recognizing where everything stood.

Having been brought up in a world where science is the ultimate arbitrator, I began to challenge myself to see if I could predict how the next alley would look, or how the view from a particular angle would appear. I kept daring myself to predict what was around every corner until I knew that something terribly strange was happening. I did not enjoy the experiments at all. I became nervous, pale, and dazed in alleys that were familiar yet not friendly. I had to come up with a reasonable answer — if there was one. It would either put me in the nuthouse, where spirits are allowed access to the present and brought about from the underworld, or unearth a logical explanation.

My final prediction was a tilted stone wall at the end of an alley near some sort of a defense tower. The wall needed to look odd — unsafe, even for the public of the old times. In my dream I had imagined arguing with the builders and pointing out the defects in their foundation, to no avail. The wall had to point to rolling hills and a green landscape visible from the tower's entrance. I went looking for it; I knew where to walk — to the left down a wide stone stairway and then to my right.

Well, there it was: a wall standing dangerously, facing the Umbrian landscape, and tilted toward a pedestrian path. It was a mental picture that I had not forgotten. At that point I broke down. Uncomfortable, overcome by emotions, and looking at the familiar stones with soggy eyes, I asked myself, "What on Earth is happening?"

I managed to find a step facing the "dangerous" wall. I had won my silly bet, but it felt very bizarre; I was not pleased at all. I kept asking myself, "What brought me over here, and how on Earth did I know how to get to this spot?" For many years I kept this story secret, except from the very close friends and family members who know how strong my mental state is.

A few years later, a friend of the family, Dr. Salwan, recommended I test my DNA with the National Geographic Society in a project called Genome Human Migration. It was amusing to see how my Y (father's side) haplogroup M35.2, having originated from Africa approximately 20,000 years ago, matched descendants of the ancients, such as Etruscans, Gauls, and Spaniards, along with North African and Levantine coastal populations. These DNA cousins, as we now call each other, are said with 97 percent certainty to have had the same grandfather twenty-five to twenty-six generations ago. I have included a table, below, showing the diverse people I matched in various countries, as well as my entire bloodline. These fascinating findings prove how close humans are, regardless of their place of origin or skin color.

On my X (mother's) side, I did not yet have any matches out of the few million or more in the database. I knew my mom was special, but not to that degree. Her haplogroup U5a was thought to have left Africa 50,000 years ago and made its way to the Near East after the melting of the last ice age; it is now most common in central and northern Europe (see map below). Maybe one day our dreams can be explained by the routes our ancestors took and places where they resided.

My "newspaper dreams" progressed as I grew up, and when I became comfortable talking about them, a good friend named Mr. Alawar recommended that I begin documenting them. He implored me to try hard at dreaming of future newspapers—if such a medium existed in the future. I kept my promise. After a few years of trying, and without warning, *voilà!*—I began reading articles dated October 13, 2046, on a black-screen background. These are the materials that prompted the making of this book.

I understand that writing books is a noble profession with certain protocols that one ought to follow: an introduction to the characters, a compelling story, and a plot with either a sad or a happy ending. Well, here I introduce the characters, but the whole book is full of plots and exciting events, thanks to the future news writers who made it possible. My introduction, as I see it, is done for pure necessity, so that readers will know the background of the scientist hero.

I came to the United States in my teens, after growing up in a household where French and Arabic were taught in schools and Arabic was spoken most often. My upbringing gave me the luxury of reading materials in these languages in addition to English, my newly acquired tongue. Newspapers in these three languages would compete in my dreams. My only wish was that one day I would remember more articles when I woke up.

I was lucky to have been given an artistic proclivity that allowed me to sculpt and paint in oil in my spare time. I chose classical subjects, usually old people and landscapes in the traditional sense; some of my work appears in this book and on the cover. My father had similar interest in art. Born in 1923, he was raised mostly by his mother. His father, Yosef, emigrated to Mexico after World War I and became a Mexican carpetbagger (*carpetbagger* is not necessarily a pejorative term in Mexico). Yosef quickly established two clothing stores, Louisa Mía ladies and Chapultepec for men. He would send money to his family to provide them with relative luxury between the world wars. Yosef died some eleven years before I was born in 1953.

My grandmother had a long, interesting life. By the time she died at age ninety-nine (1878–1977), she had witnessed the Ottoman Empire's retreat, , the famine of World War I the French conquest and free French and English occupation of World War II, and the loss of her two precious children to the infamous grippe plague in 1918 and 1919. (I remember her grief on her deathbed, which I attended as a young boy. She fervently hoped she would see Salma, age nine, and her two-year-old brother Yosef in the afterlife.) She also witnessed the first automobile rolling in the village, the first electric pole, the first telephone, and the first TV. And she recalled the first airplane that flew overhead, a double-winged contraption that she swears was so close she could see the pilot smiling.

She had her quarters in the downstairs family home, but she would often visit her other son living up the street in the next village. She always complimented their TV: "It's much better at your uncle's; I can understand everything they're saying. This TV is impolite; they speak Frangi [French] all the time" (referring to Hollywood movies and a French TV show that had some occasional kissing). As

8

a boy of twelve, I had a perfect opportunity to use some cussing language that I had learned in the village alleys. When I saw Grandma watching a passionate scene, usually with her hands over her mouth, I would stand behind the TV tube against the wall and expel the foulest language I could imagine while the foreign program was running. I pretended they could hear me and then I would ask Grandma, who was watching on the other side, "Grandma, did they stop?" She would shake her head and say, "No, those rascals." I'd repeat the cursing until she'd get embarrassed and say, "Just stop swearing, son. Turn it off. Your uncle's TV is a lot more respectful." I often recall this memory when pointing a remote control toward a TV.

The Ballouts' (pronounced "Balloot") situation improved considerably when my grandfather made it to Mexico. The money he sent allowed my dad to study accounting and then move on to positions as a teacher, a school principal in Mt. Lebanon, and a payroll officer at the ministry of education before being forced to retire in his early sixties due to the civil war. Wars had become part of the folklore in that part of the world, especially because the balance of power kept on shifting. War is not a subject of this book, although surprisingly, these days in my dreams I am reading articles from 2049 that seem not to mention a conflict in the Middle East—something for our children and grandchildren to look forward to.

But back to my grandparents. My mother lost her dad in Bolivia in 1938, when he succumbed to malaria and died alone in a wooden cabin at the age of thirty-nine. My mother and her two brothers were sent to an orphanage that was part of a school, while her mother worked the fields and relied on baking bread to feed her family with some help from her in-laws. My mother, who had a gift with numbers and an appetite for memorizing and writing poetry, became a teacher at a Catholic school near the village. She fell in love with my father in the late 1940s. Although he was outside her social rank, they married in 1952 and proceeded to produce seven children within a period of twelve years. (I was the youngest) My father had betrayed his "elite" family status, violently "ball-ed-out," and defied his relatives to marry a "commoner," a word we still use when we tease our eighty-year-old mom.

In this book I attempt to connect my dream bits in a story. I have created a proper flow to make the events as contiguous, gripping, and exciting as possible, just as I felt them in my long nightly theaters. These dreams foretell great stories, and if the articles I have "read" from the past are any indication, I think *Homo Electrus* could be very relevant in the future. I am not sure how my publisher should categorize this book. I'd hate for it to fall purely in science fiction for the reason that I do not possess all the evidence to prove today, with certainty, what can or would happen tomorrow. I certainly think that what my book describes will be the reality of the near future. Just think how within less than a hundred years, we leaped from horse buggies to space shuttles.

LA CATASTROPHE DES MINES DE COURRIÈRES

The Science;

Most of us have been taught human evolution from an early school age, and depending on the academic discipline there is a general agreement about evolution's time line. Departing from the scientific consensus are those who believe in the creation theory — that of God creating humans fully formed in our current state. Some creationists I know believe that biblical accounts do not contradict science, however. They argue that if scientists believe in a so-called abrupt theory, such as a big bang in a vacuous universe, then the spontaneous origin of man "out of nothing" is a compatible concept. I simply don't know.

But here's what we have learned from scientific study so far: About 13.7 billion years ago (plus or minus 0.17), a big bang exploded matter into a large vacuum with a radius of approximately 46 billion light years, based on comparative measurements of the neighboring hundred or so galaxies. This was confirmed by measurements of microwave radiation and the spread of particulate matter—dark, energy, and otherwise. Based on extremely reliable radiometric measurements (measuring electromagnetic radiation of uranium and lead), planet Earth was formed around 4.5 billion years ago under violent conditions. Odd cells, called anaerobic (preoxygen) cells, began to appear approximately 3.5 billion years ago. Then, 500 million years later, with the help of recently formed oxygen, organisms called prokaryotes started wiping out all the anaerobic cells. That continued for approximately 400 million years until eukaryotes (complex organisms with multiple cells) containing nuclei began to appear. Then, around 1.2 billion years ago, sex got in the way: reproduction peaked around 900 million years ago with the formation of colonies that exhibited primitive cellular specialization, leading to the first animal with a brain around 500 million years ago.

Life began getting complex. An acorn-like worm, which we call Pikaia, began showing specialization and became more advanced than its similar cousins in water. This was the first vertebrate. Then, around 400 million years ago, came the tetrapods, the first fish; the first amphibian showed up around 300 million years ago; and finally, mammals appeared around 256 million years ago. Early mammals evolved over about 250 million years and eventually appeared in a form similar to a modern dormouse. This new form, the first placental mammal, is called the eutherian.

Then, around 65 million years ago, primates appeared. They began diverging into something similar to monkeys and apes, and as they lost the ability to make their own vitamin C, they had to forage for fruits and vegetables to include it in their diet. Our branch, the hominid, diverged about 15 million years ago and entered the stages with which we are more familiar. *Homo habilis* arrived 2.5 million years ago, *Homo erectus* 1.5 million years ago, *Homo antecessor* 1.2 million years ago, and *Homo heidelbergensis* 600,000 years ago living probably along with Homo *Neanderthalensis* (Neanderthal) Finally, *Homo sapiens* appeared near Ethiopia about 160,000 to 200,000 years ago and commenced the great migrations of our ancestors.

In this book, I predict that *Homo electrus* will be next in the line of human evolution, a product of modern science's fast innovation. This shift will be swift and painful, skipping thousands if not millions of years to lose our nails, to become taller, and to form a large, egg-like head for storing compiled human teachings and added materials enabling specialization in the technically advanced world. I rely on science to explain to nonscientists how this rapid change becomes possible. It will be obvious how the foundation of this archetypal next-generation human will evolve very soon and last through the coming one thousand, ten thousand, or one million years.

My story begins with a benign research project conducted by a young scientist at Stanford. The project involves artificial memory cells combined with human DNA, XNA (synthetic DNA), and plasma on a super biomicrochip. After witnessing severe mental disabilities in children while traveling, he has decided that there must be a way to improve and empower certain areas of the brain that are affected by diseases, accidents, or simple birth defects. His research in microbiology leads him inadvertently to discover techniques that boost the brain's motor and intellectual abilities by means of an artificial implant that can be designed externally to suit each particular purpose. With a great sense of responsibility, Daniel Oakley begins investigating the interconnectivity of brain cells and improving the numerous micro electrical signals that a healthy brain is capable of making. In the process, he conducts tremendous amount of experiments and calculations, tabling the many functions and commands the brain is capable of performing in nanoseconds before getting it right.

After many long nights and great deal of arduous research and testing, Daniel has a breakthrough: he finds the proper DNA mix and develops a creative means to deliver it to a patient's damaged brain. His discovery changes his own life course and puts the entire human race through a series of tests that will alter their relationships forever. Daniel's invention brings happiness to some, sorrow to others, power to a few, and devastation to the rest. The result of this new discovery will make Evolution swift according to some scholars and stunted according to others, while the rest of the scientific community predicts the near end of civilization as we know it.

The hero goes through periods of being celebrated and famous, becoming a fugitive living in disguise, trying to do the right thing, succeeding in some instances, and failing in others. He tries desperately to remain alive while reaching out to people he trusts, becoming disappointed by many, and finding little comfort while confronting a situation from which there is no escape. He is torn between obeying the law and limiting his discovery to the very few. Should he fail to deliver his cure to the needy, or should he break the law and go out in the open, thus risking many unintended uses of his discovery?

Daniel's fame is short-lived, and his awards are insignificant in light of a new arms race by new superpowers attempting to outproduce and outmaneuver each other. Ultimately he is shunned and turned into an outcast, having realized that fulfilling his sense of destiny to become a savior and a scientific icon has been costly — perhaps deadly. What starts as a product of goodwill toward humanity's few and needy results in a must-have capability for a race unfamiliar to anyone or anything previously known.

"Life, liberty, and the pursuit of happiness" takes on a whole new meaning in the future.

Exact Y (Father) Matches

Country or Territory	Match Total	Country Total count (June 2012)
Algeria	6	890
Belarus	1	666
Côte D'Ivoire (Republic of the Ivory Coast)	1	35
Egypt	1	81
England	5	23,930
France	10	3,366
Germany	21	12,072
Hungary	1	1,181
Ireland	6	14,064
Italy	18	3,335
Lebanon	1	239
Libyan Arab Jamahiriya	2	220
Mauritania	2	2
Mexico	4	814
Morocco	13	82
Netherlands	7	1,709
Norway	1	1,335

Philippines	1	207
Poland	4	3,630
Portugal	7	786
Puerto Rico	6	242
Qatar	1	147
Russian Federation	7	3,070
Scotland	4	11,425
Somalia	1	16
Spain	49	3,351
Sweden	1	1,595
Tunisia	5	870
Ukraine	12	1,544
United Kingdom	7	10,657
United States	4	2,563
Wales	1	2,029

Haplogroup E1b1b1 is the most common variety of haplogroup among Europeans and Near Easterners. E-M78 is thought to have migrated out of Egypt 20,000 years ago. The modern population of E-M215 and E-M35 lineages are believed to have first appeared in East Africa about 22,400 years ago. Today the E1b1b1 line is most heavily represented in Mediterranean populations—approximately 12 percent of men in northern Italy, 10 percent of the men in Spain, 13 percent in central and south Italy, 20 percent of Sicily, nearly 30 percent in the Balkans and Greece, 25 percent of Jewish men, and approximately 70 percent of North Africa.

Tracing Human History Through Genetic Mutations

By examining DNA patterns that are inherited maternally or paternally, scientists can trace human lineages back to the original branches, or sons and daughters, of a genetic Adam and an Eve.

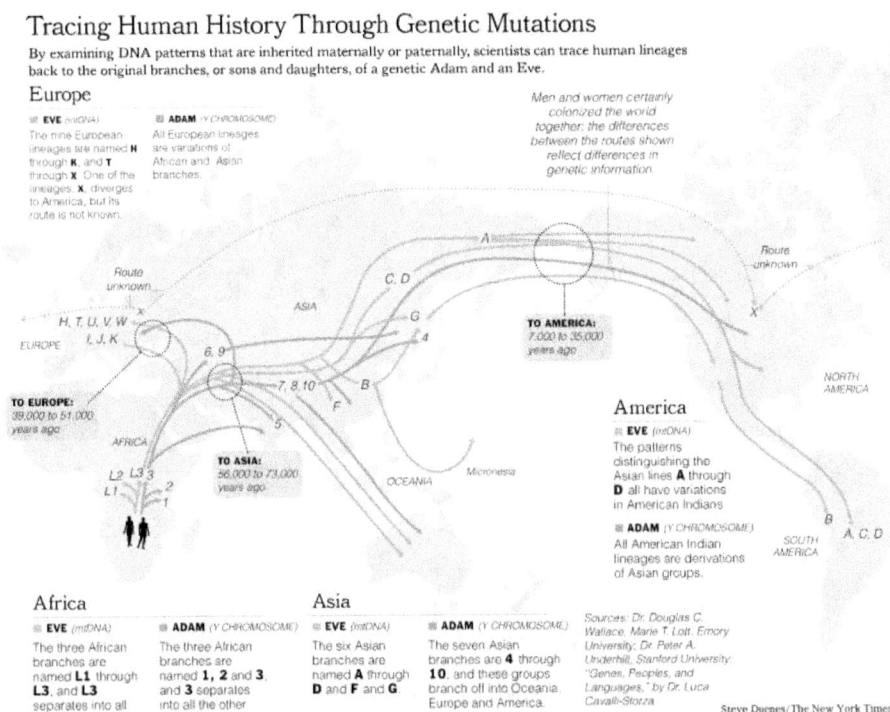

Europe

EVE *(mtDNA)*
The nine European lineages are named **H** through **K**, and **T** through **X**. One of the lineages, **X**, diverges to America, but its route is not known.

ADAM *(Y CHROMOSOME)*
All European lineages are variations of African and Asian branches.

Men and women certainly colonized the world together; the differences between the routes shown reflect differences in genetic information

Route unknown

H, T, U, V, W
I, J, K

EUROPE

6, 9

7, 8, 10

5

AFRICA

TO EUROPE:
39,000 to 51,000 years ago

TO ASIA:
56,000 to 73,000 years ago

L2 L3 3
L1 2
1

ASIA

C, D

G

4

B

F

OCEANIA

Micronesia

TO AMERICA:
7,000 to 35,000 years ago

Route unknown

X

NORTH AMERICA

America

EVE *(mtDNA)*
The patterns distinguishing the Asian lines **A** through **D** all have variations in American Indians

ADAM *(Y CHROMOSOME)*
All American Indian lineages are derivations of Asian groups.

SOUTH AMERICA

B
A, C, D

Africa

EVE *(mtDNA)*
The three African branches are named **L1** through **L3**, and **L3** separates into all the other branches

ADAM *(Y CHROMOSOME)*
The three African branches are named **1, 2** and **3**, and **3** separates into all the other branches

Asia

EVE *(mtDNA)*
The six Asian branches are named **A** through **D** and **F** and **G**

ADAM *(Y CHROMOSOME)*
The seven Asian branches are **4** through **10**, and these groups branch off into Oceania, Europe and America.

Sources: Dr. Douglas C. Wallace, Marie T. Lott, Emory University; Dr. Peter A. Underhill, Stanford University; "Genes, Peoples, and Languages," by Dr. Luca Cavalli-Storza

Steve Duenes/The New York Times

U Group (Mother's side). Haplogroup U5 is the most common in western and northern Europe.

DNA tests on ancient skeletons have shown that U5 was a principal mitochondrial haplogroup of Paleolithic and Mesolithic hunter-gatherers in northern Europe. Ancient DNA tests conducted in Britain, Germany, and Scandinavia indicate that the frequency of U5 has progressively declined over time through the Neolithic population, the Bronze Age, the Iron Age, and the Middle Ages. Nowadays it remains most common in the far north of Europe, where the Mesolithic population has been least affected by subsequent migrations. For instance, 30 to 50 percent of the Sami people of northern Scandinavia belong to U5b (and about 40 percent to haplogroup V, which is also of pre-Neolithic European origin).

Chapter 1

An Unusual Family

Daniel was born to an ordinary family. He had one brother and one sister. His father, Robert, worked in his own architectural firm, and his mother, Ama, was a capable housewife who had found her calling as the star of a cooking show. Despite her career, his mother remained attentive to her household. She would review the kids' homework, while Robert would occasionally intervene with an illustrative example, a historical fact, or even a PowerPoint presentation. Fascinated by his mother's cooking from an early age, Daniel would watch her prepare the ingredients and make precise portions of the various Mediterranean foods she prepared. She had studied economics and was precise with her measurements; she did not tolerate any guesswork and had very low error margins in her recipes. As a small child Daniel would sit on his knees near the kitchen sink and watch and learn, while Mom would occasionally let him try one mixture or another. She would ask his opinion, which at the age of two consisted mostly of facial expressions that may or may not have been relevant to the dish.

As he grew older, he began helping with the tedious preparation of portions that were needed for the camera. When the crew came to film, he would have all the ingredients laid out on the table, and he would explain what they were and when they were added to the pot. Following the advice of their family attorney and brother-in-law, Edward, his mom had a policy not to let her children be filmed for safety reasons. Her husband enjoyed the spotlight a lot more than his wife did. When he was occasionally invited on camera, he would seize the opportunity to bring up his architectural business and list the highlights of past or current projects. He would drop names like Bellagio, Fifth Avenue, and New York City.

Daniel's older siblings Alexander and Laura were of different nature. They enjoyed the arts and excelled in drawings and music. They had their chance to entertain the film crew before their mother's show, *Ama's Cooking,* began.

Daniel started asking difficult questions at an early age. At five years old he asked who created God, and his parents stumbled to answer. That evening his father proposed that he ask Sister Alessandra at school the next day. Daniel later answered his own question with a most profound idea: "I think God created himself."

Daniel also enjoyed adding and subtracting numbers. He would ask how many seconds there were in a day or a year, how far away the stars were, how many steps a person walked per day, or how many people were in attendance at a party. He would count white, red, and blue cars on the way to Lake Tahoe when the family would take a weekend vacation. Daniel had a great vocabulary that he would show off in the car while playing word games. He kept his older brother and sister on their toes by reciting the many different bones and other parts of the body. He had a loving character, and, unlike most kids, he enjoyed hugging his grandparents and family and friends who visited.

Daniel's disdain for sweets was a remarkable trait inherited from his father. An unusually healthy eater, he was twelve years old before he tried chocolate. He was soon at the top of his class and was thrilled to be accepted at Stanford University for an undergraduate program in microbiology, with a double major in microphysics. At Stanford he earned a master's degree and graduated with honors. He would always comment to his friends, "The more you learn, the more you realize how little you know."

Daniel in the kitchen

Daniel's parents were aging, and although they lived very close to his studio apartment in Palo Alto, he felt guilty about not being able to see them very often. He would politely decline most invitations, even when his mother would cook his favorite dish. It was a big treat when the entire family would meet at Thanksgiving and Christmas. Occasionally Daniel would take a schoolmate or, on rare occasions, a girlfriend to introduce to the family.

Daniel's sister Laura was an accomplished veterinarian working in a small partnership in San Jose. She was happily married to David Homer, a soft-spoken scientist who worked for a pharmaceutical company in South San Francisco, and they lived in Woodside, halfway between the two major cities of the Bay Area. Laura had an artistic side; she loved playing the piano and had a good hand for drawing her favorite characters in watercolor.

His brother Alex was an archaeologist with a degree from UC Berkeley. He laid claim to discovering sarcophaguses in the Levant and deciphering weathered inscriptions that were buried in the sediment of Mount Kneisset, Lebanon. His discoveries had pushed back the time line of the northern Hittites' expansion by about five hundred years on the Phoenician coast. They were deemed so important, that his 'papers' were published by the National Geographic Society (among others) and were translated in over twenty languages. Nevertheless, he had his doubters and critics. Alex was married to a Macedonian woman named Sonia, whom he had met in college; she was an attorney specializing in patent law in San Francisco.

Alexander at the site of his newly discovered ancient writings near Mt. Kneisset, Lebanon.

Chapter 2

Egypt: Titan's Inspiration

Christmas 2045 was unusually mild. Alex's parents received the good news that Sonia was pregnant. Joy was in the air. Alex's mom was especially happy that she had been told before Olga, Sonia's mother. It seems that during Thanksgiving Sonia had hesitated to tell her parents in order to avoid the melodrama for which her mom was famous. At Christmas dinner, Laura and Alex recalled visiting Egypt while they were young. Although Daniel had also been there, he had been only four years old, so he struggled to remember anything relevant except for the sight of the pyramids. They decided on the spot that the entire family should try for a second visit; this time it would be a lot more meaningful and would include their aging parents on all sides. The plan was set for September 2046, when the new baby would be five months old and ready to travel, and when the weather in Egypt would be best. Planning the trip that year took a toll on the family, as there were conflicting schedules and deadlines. Daniel could go for only a week, and Sonia's mother was unable to fly due to a stroke that had left her left side partially paralyzed.

When in the end they met at Cairo's airport on September 27, 2046, they had all taken separate airlines from the United States. Daniel's family had been onboard for six and a half hours — a relatively short flight from San Francisco aboard a new 1,210-passenger Boeing jet called B2020A, operated by United Airlines. They had organized their stay at the Four Seasons Hotel downtown, the same place where Daniel and his family had stayed over twenty-five years ago.

The Oakleys on their first trip to Egypt

Driving to the heart of the city, the family discovered that the earlier chaos they had encountered did not seem to have changed. On the surface, the infrastructure of Cairo appeared modern; roads and bridges across the Nile were well kept, the roads were wide, and the avenues were well lit. The only problem was that the population of Egypt, which was close to 100 million, lived mostly around the fertile Nile River and was concentrated in the only two metropolises of Alexandria and Cairo (the latter had 35 million inhabitants within its suburbs alone). The canals that Muhammad Ali built in the 1820s to expand the city and to improve the irrigation system were just as wide as they had been originally — though the heavy garbage, combined with the morbid smell of dead animals, likely had not been present in the 1800s. The family celebrated in style, and Alex and Sonia's baby Perla tolerated the mild heat of eighty five degrees Fahrenheit.

After doing the routine bus tours to the pyramids at Giza and spending a day at Cairo's newly built Egyptian national museum, they were ready to take a Nile cruise aboard a luxury boat with sleeping quarters to the southern part of the

Valley of the Kings near Aswan. The three-day trip promised to have excellent accommodations and to be comfortable enough for guests to withstand the desert heat.

The daily tours went well, and there was a good family dynamic, except when Robert, Daniel's father, would plague the young tour guide with overbearing questions. Mirvet, the guide, was a recent college graduate in history from Cairo University. She looked like Nefertiti, with large, black eyes and soft, pale skin, and though she was well spoken, she lacked both understanding and interest in Robert's sarcastic jokes. He had a troublesome habit of showing off his historical knowledge. At home, his wife dealt with this by having him sit and read in the kitchen corner while she prepared her ingredients for her many TV appearances—an arrangement that kept the peace. (Robert once complained to his wife, "When do I get to correct people if you keep making me read?" Thus, showing his knowledge of ancient history to the poor tour guide was just part of the bargain. Mirvet took it well, as it was part of her job; she had seen many foreigners come and go. Some were fascinated with local history, while others were disappointed with the country's shabby appearance away from the metropolis and overwhelmed by the visible struggle of the people.

Daniel was unusually timid, and he would not make eye contact with Mirvet. For her part, she gave him an occasional quick glance but never attempted direct eye contact. She seemed comfortable and confident with everyone, skilled in communication, and presumably refined as a result of coming into contact with some of the millions of tourists that flocked to Egypt every year. Besides, she had likely taken classes in tourism offices in order to build these very skills. Mirvet seemed to have all the answers for everything, and she was remarkably good at combining previous questions with new ones. She did have a few quirks, such as yelling out for everyone to listen, as if her charges were in grammar school. On rare occasions she would look at one of the tourists, a Japanese lady, and say, "I will have a better answer for you later," when Daniel, being attentive to details, would swear that the tourist hadn't asked anything.

Mirvet asked Daniel what he did, or if he was still in college. He answered that he worked in labs where he looked at cells and DNA and conducted boring experiments, that he preferred what she did, and that he dreaded how short the Egypt trip was. "One week in Egypt is not enough," she said. He replied that he had begun a very important experiment on lab animals and could not afford to stay longer; it could set him back months and delay his PhD.

Mirvet took a liking to Daniel, whose questions were few but very different from the rest. He would ask about the population size of each little town they passed, the people's source of income, the average family size, the average home's square footage, and the presence of a historical discovery. The modern boat had a forty-five-passenger capacity. Most of them straddled on the balconies, walked up and down, switched sides, and took pictures. They finally arrived at the Valley of the Kings and, after a brief introduction to the passengers, got off the boat.

Daniel chose to walk next to Mirvet, who continued trying to make conversation by asking him if he liked what he was doing and if his studies were interesting. He replied that he was not going to waste this precious vacation time trying to explain his lab; it was full of testing equipment that was used to look closer and closer at everything around us — "Down to the atom level, if that helps" — and he preferred that she keep talking about Egypt. She teased him about how rude he was, and both burst into a giddy laugh. They appeared to be softly smitten with one another, but neither dared to make the first move, or even to make the slightest overture — at least in public. Mirvet kept explaining the dates, circumstances, habits, and afflictions of every dead king. Daniel would nod but rarely talk.

The boat was docked in the Blue Nile Company's pier number 3. The bedrooms for the guides were on the lower floor, without any apparent windows looking onto the river, but the tourists enjoyed a great view and surprisingly spacious accommodations on the top levels. The middle was reserved for the restaurant and reception, where every night at dinner a belly dancer would entertain the guests by flopping her belly and her behind to the sound of old Egyptian classical music. The dancer was not the most athletic, but she had a pretty face, and you could notice the flapping of her skin as she visibly tried to keep a smile at all times as if she were in pain. It had remained a tradition in North Africa that a little fat on the extremities was a sign of good health that ought to be preserved. (Alex remarked that belly dancing ought to be called butt dancing instead, a joke that busted the entire party into a loud, obnoxious laugh.) During act two, while the main course was being served, a male dervish dancer ornamented with LED lights would appear and dazzle the crowd with his remarkable dance. As a special effect, he would turn his lights on and off in a perfect sequence with the music. They would shine on his jacket, on his tarboosh, and finally on his skirt as he swirled in place like a UFO hovering over the dance floor. He'd keep at it for about a half hour, without stopping and without getting dizzy.

There was one last excursion away from the Nile before heading back to Cairo: the program called for a visit to a local museum and traditional rug-making factory in the town of Arid, about fifteen miles away from the Nile. Minivans took the interested passengers to show them the bonus of local village life and customs. At first glance the museum appeared to be a minimarket or a retail store, with a front parking lot and a great big sign suited more for a business than for a museum. Mirvet's explanation was that the mayor of this poor town was the owner of a few local markets and, to help his constituents and fellow citizens, he had donated one of them to the municipality so that they could transform it into a museum. This made it appear a noble gift in addition to explaining its appearance. It would have been unfair to judge the motives of the mayor; it seemed he had done the right thing, and the local inhabitants seemed to be pleased with the gesture—and thus likely to reelect him.

The fact that a neglected village had a patron was definitely cause for celebration. After all, some U.S. towns and cities, especially on the West Coast, had been founded in the early 1800s with the help of a patron. The locals in Arid were kind not only to tourists, but also to each other. For instance, Laura witnessed a man helping a street vendor reload his vegetable cart after it was toppled. The vendor tried in vain to give the man potatoes or even money, but the man vehemently refused and instead gave the vendor a big hug. Laura managed to capture a video of the incident and showed it to our party.

The museum was dark, but as soon as the minivan pulled in, the place lit up and the air-conditioning came on. The scattered parties were then courteously greeted and shown the ancient rugs hung on the walls. According to the guides, the rugs, some of which were framed in Plexiglas, dated as far back as a thousand years. The quality looked to be above average, and some appeared to be as fine as the famous Chinese silk rugs worth over a million dollars, or 100 thousand G currency (the newly adopted currency that was backed by commodities, 1G is equivalent to ten U.S dollars). There were also shelves decorated with stone figurines and some old plowing tools and shovels that dated back millennia.

At the back corner of the museum, visible to all, a sign with the words FACTORY DOWNSTAIRS flashed intermittent light and begged visitors' curiosity. Daniel looked at the sign and asked if he could go there. He seemed to have taken the bait: two individuals rushed to assist him and showed him the dim corridor leading downstairs. "Let's go down, guys!" Daniel yelled. Though his parents hesitated, Laura and Alex obliged, and soon the entire party was forming in single file, ready to go downstairs. The guide delivered an apology for "zis crazy light," but soon the entire staircase was lit and the way to the "factory" was open.

Laura carrying her niece, Perla

At first glance the visitors saw thin threads hanging on wooden frames approximately eight feet wide by six feet tall, dropping about four feet from the ceiling above each worker's station. "Wait!" Laura shouted. "Guys, there are kids working here!"

She was right. Children aged about six to twelve had genuine smiles on their faces as they labored at complex designs. Some showed extraordinary skills, handling two or more threads at once and 'packing' the string that would eventually make up a rug. The young laborers would meticulously follow the patterns, which were marked in vertical lines.

Children weaving rugs in Asyut

The basement appeared clean and well organized, with a lamp shining above each station. Laura asked the museum "salesman" about the local laws allowing kids to work in the factory at such a young age. The explanation was that they went to school until 1:30 p.m., and then they worked at the museum from 3 until 7. It was perfectly legal; the government allowed it as a way to support the large families of Egypt's interior. For the strategy to work, the "salesman" pointed out, the museum desperately needs to sell the children's rugs.

"Not all kids qualify," he remarked. "There is a long waiting list at the front desk. The museum rotates families and their children to allow everyone in need a chance to earn money on the side, as a way to improve their lives and boost the family's income. Kids with disabilities will always have priority, however. They don't have to be from the village if they can perform the work."

He introduced the party to a seven-year-old boy who appeared to be paraplegic but was extremely capable. His already fast weaving speed accelerated when the visitors approached him. The station beside him was reserved for a ten-year-old girl who had some sort of neural or muscular disorder. Although she was unable to speak, she managed to smile at the tourists as she moved her tiny fingers on a small-scale platform. Daniel, although impressed, was visibly shaken at the sight of this little girl. Mirvet was unusually kind to her: she hugged and kissed her on the cheek and spoke to her in Arabic. The girl nodded her head in agreement. Before Daniel had a chance to ask, Mirvet said that the girl was named Sara, and she was from a town near Cairo that Mirvet knew well. Daniel was heartbroken at such a sight. Sara had long eyelashes and an innocent look, and she wore a pink cotton dress that looked too big for her. It was very painful to look at her, yet Daniel was fascinated by how she and the other kids were able to follow complex patterns and weave at extraordinary speed fine rugs that could be displayed in luxury stores worldwide. He knew the basics about rugs—for instance, the finer the thread, the more they were worth—and with such tiny fingers packing the strings, they certainly gave child labor an added value and a whole new meaning. The fact that modern machines could do the same job flawlessly was viewed as a disadvantage to refined clients looking for subtle thread errors, usually found in the back of the rug.

The visit ended at the opposite end of the basement, at the top of the staircase, where large stacks of rugs of various size and quality were sold to benefit the children. Visitors bought what they could after minimal negotiation with the museum salespeople. The guilt was way too much to bear, so tourists paid up and shut up.

The tourists spent their last night on the boat heading back to Cairo. Daniel had grown anxious and irritable. He began complaining about the food and claimed he had a headache due to all the work waiting for him at the lab. He tried to explain to his parents that he was investigating a new virus called M13, a bacteriophage, which was harmless to humans but could generate power through converting movement into electricity, a property called Piozoelectric. His mother responded, "Wear gloves. And don't let those things get into your blood." Daniel's work was so complicated that the rest of the family didn't even ask questions; his worry seemed legitimate.

Daniel felt different later that night, however. After everyone went to bed, he went up near the control room to get a glance at the wavy shorelines of the Nile and the distant farms and villages. The moonlight made it possible to see the mounds of pigeon towers, which were made of mud and erratically thrown about in the field. The pigeons served a great purpose: they ate insects and kept the wild birds from eating the locally grown food. Daniel sat on a ledge with his back to the control room, dangled his feet, and threaded his hands through the middle of a double chrome railing. He thought about what he had seen at the museum, the poor little girl working, his lab work at Stanford, his parents, and, yes, Mirvet. He could not bear to accept that his feelings were taking over his actions. As a man of science, he was fighting his desire to see her, but he was losing. Instead, emotions would rule the evening: he really wanted to see her, to touch her, and—why not?—a passionate kiss wouldn't hurt. And if she wanted to continue talking about Egypt, well then, let it be. He could not get her out of his mind, knowing that in the next twenty-four hours he'd be thousands of miles away and regretting not having at least tried. "Something should be done, and quickly," he thought.

Daniel began to move—but wait! Mirvet was walking right below him. Where was she going, and what was she up to? She walked cautiously, looking over her shoulder as she leaned to grab something from a toolbox. Daniel ducked out of sight.

Mirvet kept walking, this time with a lot more confidence, and Daniel decided to follow. He jumped ever so softly onto the lower deck. He could see that she had taken the narrow staircase on the kitchen side, leading toward the cook's cabin, but then she had taken another turn and disappeared in the hallway that led the other way, to the storeroom. The lights were dim. Daniel recalled another staircase leading further down to the employees' cabins. He kept going; although he had lost sight of Mirvet, he was sure that she had gone in that direction. His emotions had put him on a blind chase. He was insistent on finding her and desperate to have a private conversation with her.

The sound of the engine was getting louder as Daniel kept walking toward the engine compartment. There was a faint diesel smell coming from the machinery. He realized that he had lost track of Mirvet, and just as he paused, he felt a sharp, sudden stab just below his right shoulder. He let out an agonizing cry for help that could be heard throughout the boat.

The Blue Nile boat.

Daniel leaned against the corridor walls as he staggered from one side of the hall to the other. He ended up at the bottom of the staircase, on his knees and desperate for help. The first person to arrive was Captain Naji, who took both of Daniel's arms and tried dragging his body to the top of the staircase, then Daniel slowly shifted, revealing an object sticking out of his back. The captain yelled for help, as they were stuck at the stairs leading up to the kitchen. Everyone scrambled, and soon the entire boat was filled with panicked passengers and rumors that the boat was sinking. A mechanic and a cook appearing rough and unshaved like convicts, grabbed Daniel's feet, and began carrying him to the main hall. Robert stood at the top of a narrow staircase and watched in panic as the men carried his son on their shoulders. "Daniel, Daniel!" Robert cried. He had recognized his son's loud yell for help while on one of his occasional strolls to smoke a cigar, but he hadn't known which direction to go.

Robert found Daniel struggling to breathe. He grabbed his son's arm and saw blood everywhere. Turning him on his side exposed a dirty yellow handle belonging to a screwdriver that had penetrated Daniel's rib cage. "We need a doctor!" Robert yelled. "Someone stabbed my son!"

It all seemed to take forever. Daniel's mom, Ama, was not around; her small dose of wine that evening had guaranteed a good night's sleep. Unaware of the commotion downstairs, she slept soundly—for now.

"We are close to Asyut," said Captain Naji. He had radioed the police there and informed them of the incident. But Robert would hear none of it. He demanded that a helicopter take his son to the nearest hospital and threatened to shoot the captain if he didn't comply. Robert had no gun and was nowhere near one, but the sight of his bloody son had almost taken him to the edge, and he appeared dangerous enough. The captain could be heard screaming on his radio, "Ayezz et chopper tae elessaf delwati, wella he ysir magzara!" ("I need a medic chopper now or a massacre will take place!")

The quiet Japanese couple appeared, and the wife called Hedeco startled everyone by yelling, "Away, away!" and beginning to give orders. She took charge and commanded the crowd with her broken English. She was wearing a white robe and appeared to have white paste on her face and began asking for clean towels and alcohol in a firm manner, giving the impression that she either was a doctor or was certainly familiar with such emergencies.

Meanwhile, Daniel's brother and sister were doing a good job comforting their wounded sibling. Alex kept repeating, "You're not going to die; it's a surface wound.' His sister was saying, "Look, your heart is on the other side. You'll make it; trust me." Hedeco, whose nickname was now the Nurse, made the crowd stand back and proclaimed that Daniel's right lung was punctured. She proceeded to cover the stab wound and applied pressure so that the bleeding practically stopped—she knew not to try and remove the screwdriver. Hedeco turned Daniel on the opposite side so the wound would be above his heart and gravity would help the flow of blood work in his favor. Daniel was mostly coherent; he tried answering his father's query as to who had stabbed him by saying that it had been dark and that he had not seen anyone. The captain kneeled and asked Daniel what he had been doing in the area reserved for employees, and Daniel mumbled something to the effect that he had been lost. He must have said the words "I don't know" a hundred times.

Soon the helicopter sounded overhead, and the captain and first officer, Issa, began to argue about the safety of landing a chopper on the boat. The first officer suggested they dock somewhere close for the helicopter to pick up the injured man. Captain Naji argued that the boat was plenty sturdy and equipped with a landing area, Issa contended that the "crazy contraption" had not been tried before. In the end, the captain stuck to his guns. He assured everyone that his boat, made in Germany by Bavaria Motor Boats, was only four years old and would readily withstand the landing of an ambulance chopper.

At this moment, Daniel's mother appeared and started a frantic cry.

"What's happening here?!" she said. Her kids, aware of their mother's sensitivity, assured her that all was okay, that Daniel had fallen and may have broken his leg, and that he needed to be in a hospital. Their subterfuge did not work: there was a pool of blood, and everyone seemed to have blood on his hands. It appeared Ama's family had underestimated her, however; she calmly asked Laura what had happened and was able to hear the truth. Ama whispered to Robert that she would fly with Daniel, who was already being carried away on a stretcher. Robert disagreed and said that he should go. Alex finally settled the matter: his parents would both stay on the boat, and he would accompany his brother to the hospital and stay in touch with them.

Surprisingly, the chopper was not very loud when it landed. Soon afterward the two young medics showed up. Decked in all sorts of gear, they appeared to be well trained for the mission. They had spoken briefly to Hedeco and had agreed on a method for transporting Daniel.

Asyut, a city with a population of about five million, was situated halfway between the Valley of the Kings, near Aswan, and Cairo. Recently it had become famous for the discovery of the hidden city of Mamun. A satellite had spied this ancient city's outlines in 2015, and the government, with rare speed, had excavated it within five years. Mamun was the capital city of the early pharaoh Actun in the third millennium BC. It later became known as the Pompeii of the Desert, (original being in the south of Italy) except for the dead, calcified bodies. Everything appeared to be modern from the air. Asyut seemed to glow everywhere; the roads and bridges shone, and bright lights were reflected in the shape of an entangled octopus. All of this was made possible with the wealth of natural gas with which Egypt recently had been blessed. The discovery of a large natural-gas reservoir near Luxor in 2015 had improved the national economy and had helped quell the fanatical inclination of the poorer population.

Sabag Hospital had been built twenty-five years earlier, when the United States was subsidizing peace in the region by paying billions of dollars to the governments of the eastern Mediterranean. Daniel was admitted to the emergency room, where doctors removed the screwdriver, stitched him back up, and drained his lung, which had suffered a severe puncture. Finally, he was given a heavy course of antibiotics and a dose of Ketoprofen 20mg painkiller pills. Daniel also had lost a lot of blood, and he needed four units. Alex supplied two of them, as the brothers shared an A-positive blood type. By now the boat had docked in Asyut, and everyone welcomed the news of Daniel's successful surgery. The captain had initiated an investigation of the incident, and the local police had entrusted a local magistrate inspector to get to the bottom of it. A story like this needed to be resolved. It was bad for business, bad for tourism, and even worse for Asyut to have an incident like this seen on TV or heard everywhere on RadGio, an open advertisement radio platform that enables private broadcasting and messaging besides accessing the multitude radio stations worldwide.

Even the mayor had visited the boat with an entourage suitable for heads of state, including excessive security. A short, stubby man wearing large sunglasses and a white suit, the mayor looked like Poirot of the 1990s TV series, but with a bigger belly. After being chased by a small local news crew van, he decided to give the media an update outside the boat's entrance, with the vessel's name— *Blue Nile*—as his backdrop. Before anyone could ask him a question, he began: "Ze situation is now underztood. We have a lead zat will lead us to ze criminal. I can say no more because of ze investigation, you see. . . ."

The two news reporters were lead away by bodyguards, and the mayor turned his attention to the boat. "Zis is beautiful. Why should anyone hurt anyone on zis boat? Is too beautiful here."

Stuck on the boat, the local magistrate had asked everyone to gather in the restaurant, with guards at both entrances, and asked if anybody wished for an attorney to be present before he began his questioning—a smart move on his part, as a person requesting an attorney usually had something to hide, at least in theory. Egypt had come a long way since the days of President Musa, who reinstituted a British system of government whose seeds were planted in the previous century. Corruption remained, however, and it was especially prominent in rural areas. The farther you got from the city, the less present the government appeared to be; for example, people in the country would settle their disputes with traditional local justice that varied from compensating victims to serving jail time to flogging—but rarely a death sentence. No one on the boat asked for an attorney to be present, so the magistrate proceeded to take them all one by one to the captain's quarters for questioning.

Mirvet, very composed and alert, had sat next to Robert and Ama and asked the guard how long they had to be onboard. The guard, a tall, dark man by the name of Amr, answered in a loud voice, *"Maarafsh"* ("I don't know").

Egypt's population has always been a curiosity to visitors. The closer one is to the Mediterranean coastal cities, especially Alexandria and Damietta, the lighter the skin of the people. Historians have argued that lighter-skinned Egyptians are descended from the Greek colonies during the days of Ptolemy and Cleopatra, and they were added to a Middle Eastern population influx during the Islamic expansion in 640 AD. The people of the interior and the south have darker complexions owing to African influence; they are likely the descendents of pyramid builders during the various pharaohs' projects. Amr appeared to be from central Africa rather than Egypt, yet he spoke Arabic and was a pure Egyptian. The country is ancient enough that its people have ceased to see color; thankfully, racism has long been forgotten. One can see all kinds of shades on the full spectrum of employment.

Mirvet had finished her turn being interviewed and waited for Robert to return to the hallway. She whispered to Robert that his son might not have been the intended victim of the assault. She guessed that the perpetrator had to be exceptionally strong, and she felt the police ought to quiz the only strong man on the boat: the cook. She had said as much to the police chief, but he apparently ignored her advice; he wanted to question everyone on the ship about where they were at the time of the attack — "even if I find rats that can talk," he said. The chief had gotten agitated after being told there were no fingerprints or meaningful DNA samples on the screwdriver. All the towels used for blocking the wound, along with Daniel's subsequent treatment in the ER, had compromised some of the evidence. Mirvet had admitted to the police and the family that she had been on the lower deck just before the crime and that she had walked back to her room at about the same time she heard Daniel's scream.

Overall, though, the investigation was going nowhere. Hedeco and her husband were the last to be interviewed. They were questioned at the same time; her husband spoke neither English nor Arabic, so Hedeco acted as an English translator. The surprising fact that Hedeco had tended to Daniel's wound, despite not being a doctor or a nurse and having no prior experience with injuries, was extraordinary. As she explained to the police, she had saved Daniel's life by relying only on knowledge gleaned from reading novels and from watching movies — an incredible feat for an ordinary woman. Like Mirvet, Hedeco theorized that the cook had done it. She told the police chief that she could see in his eyes that he was guilty.

Alex called his parents and told them the good news: Daniel had been saved and would be allowed to fly back to the United States in two days. Upon hearing the good news, the police did not press the investigation much further. Their suspicion lay with the janitor with the speech impediment. Although he had no detectable motive, and everyone on board knew the poor soul was innocent, he seemed to have both the necessary strength and a tendency to lose his temper. In addition, he had no ability to defend himself and recount his location on the boat at the time of the attack. All the police chief could do was take him to the station and keep him for few days; having failed to get a confession, the police released the janitor twenty-four hours later, after he agreed to sign a pledge never to work aboard ships again, thus satisfying Egyptian justice. He walked away crying and cursing in his mumbled speech. It broke everyone's heart in Asyut.

Chapter 3

The Breakthrough

Daniel's recovery was quick. It took him only three extra days to resume his lab work. His colleagues were happy to see him alive — especially his aging professors, Keith Mathieson, a pioneer of the wireless retinal implant, and Seung-Wuk Lee, inventor of a biogenerator.

Dr. Mathieson had made a breakthrough back in 2012, when he was able to combine a prosthetic microchip (retinal photoreceptor chip) with a photovoltaic silicon ship similar to a tiny solar panel and implant the device in the back of the eye, where it acted as pair of glasses. The device was fitted with a video camera that recorded what was happening before a patient's eyes and fired beams of near-infrared light onto the retinal chip. This created an electrical signal that was passed on to the nerves, thus making it possible to restore sight to the blind.

Although Daniel was relatively young, he had helped during the previous year's master's program in biophysics and, with a fellow student named Richard Wilson, set the record for wireless data transmission in the terahertz band (known as T-rays) by beating a Japanese team in the yotta speed of 1,000Y (1Y=100GB/sec). (Terahertz waves penetrate many materials as effectively as X-rays do but deposit far less energy and therefore cause less damage.)

Before coming to Stanford, Daniel's other professor, Seung-Wuk Lee, had developed a "generator" from a virus-based electrode that converted mechanical movements, such as tapping a finger, into electricity in a process known as piezoelectricity.

Daniel's thesis in progress was based on expanding Dr. Lee's discovery by investigating a new virus called M26 bacteriophage, which attacks bacteria but is benign to humans. Daniel used a genetic-engineering technique to add thirteen negatively charged molecules to one end of corkscrew-shaped proteins that coated the virus. These additional molecules increased the charge difference between the proteins' positive and negative ends, thus boosting the electrical charge of the virus. The advantage of using viruses for such tasks was that they arranged themselves into an orderly film that enabled the "generator" to work and to produce higher voltage. This attribute, known as self-assembly, was the main goal in the field of nanotechnology and could be used one day for neurorehabilitation, or mending severed nerves, in cases such as spinal cord injury.

Back in the lab, Daniel was unable to shake the memory of Egypt from his head — his injury, the disabled children at the museum, and Mirvet. He had a sense of unfinished business, and he kept thinking of ways to improve the lives of the children at the rug factory. He had had a relatively sheltered upbringing; his family was not very adventurous, and they would always choose safe places for their yearly vacations. The closest he had come to any danger or disturbance was when he was three years old. While his family was on a trip to Istanbul in July 2026, a massive protest by union workers and government employees had broken out into full riots, because Turkey had agreed to austerity measures recommended by the European Union. The Oakleys had been stuck in a downtown hotel while police officers in riot gear had shot rubber bullets at protesters and dragged away the blood-soaked injured, some to the very hotel where the family was trapped. The riots had ended near the hotel district but continued elsewhere, thus providing enough time for tourists to be escorted to the piers, then by small boats in rough seas to Greece in a journey that made more headlines in the United States than what was happening in Istanbul. The airport remained shut down for a period of time, so the family took a military transport back to the United States via Dublin. The U.S. State Department had arranged the transport for U.S. nationals caught in the riot—mostly those of Turkish origin.

That lesson had been enough for Daniel's parents to choose safer and more stable places to go on holiday in the summers. When Daniel was in his teens the family had visited interesting places like Brazil and Mexico, where he had seen kids suffering and begging on street corners, but he had never come close to witnessing disabled children laboring. Egypt would continue to haunt him.

What if he could help? Maybe he could use the new 5hmC (5-hydroxymethylcytosine, at the 5th position in the mammalian genome) and make a brain prosthesis with modified DNA. Could he deviate from the dissertation that he was to submit to Dr. Lee? Would the professor agree? What if he could identify the children's defective genes and replace them with healthier genes of identical sequence? For instance, he could mix their DNA with 5hmC, which was known to help activate healthier genes, and potentially cure these patients. Scientists had been working on the common 5mC (DNA methylation) that does the opposite—silences or turns off genes. That method, pioneered by Dr. Dan Mattock at Genentech, had been very successful in arresting tumor growth and the spread of lymphoma in cancer patients for over twenty years.

Daniel had barely slept on that busy Tuesday, when everyone seemed to call him. He kept asking himself "what if" questions, considering every tiny inquiry he could think of, and brainstorming possible solutions. That Wednesday, October 14, 2046, he left early and rushed to Dr. Lee's office on the south side of the microbiology building, known as the Fairchild Building. He knew Dr. Lee was an early riser and normally would be reviewing papers and preparing for his lectures. Daniel found him speaking on the phone with a colleague named Paolo Torres at the Polytechnic University of Milan. That university had caused what was termed a cultural earthquake back in 2014, when it had instituted a policy requiring that courses be taught in English only. Soon most technical schools throughout the world had followed suit, except for those in China, where pride would not allow it. The Chinese had recently surpassed the U.S. GDP and had switched to the G currency after the world market collapse of March 2038. The G currency, which eventually was adopted worldwide, began taking hold in 2031, after the United States established a timetable to switch to it within ten years. In frenzy, countries began to replace their national currencies. They forewent FIAT currencies — those no longer backed by a gold standard — thus providing stability to financial institutions throughout the world and relying on real commodities to value the G.

Dr. Lee got off the phone and listened to Daniel's new ideas about changing course on his dissertation. Daniel requested that he switch to working on the 5hmC and promised that Dr. Lee could be a co inventor if his new method worked. There was no protocol that made Stanford University a beneficiary partner and arbitrator of any invention within its walls, but, Daniel said, he needed Dr. Lee's guidance and wished that his work be kept secret. Dr. Lee started to quiz Daniel intensely on the subject. He asked very difficult questions, but Daniel surprisingly had most, if not all, the answers. Dr. Lee promised to give Daniel his decision by the following day at about the same time.

Leaving Dr. Lee's office, Daniel seemed to be walking on clouds. He felt that he was on the cusp of something very big: a new technique in genome biology that would change the lives of disabled people worldwide, especially children.

The next day, Dr. Lee approved of Daniel's new direction and conceded that his idea may indeed have merits. Dr. Lee directed Daniel to provide a weekly progress report.

Daniel got to work immediately. He structured the experiments that he needed to do, established the direction that he ought to follow, and resolved to keep an open mind for any results that would change the entire course of his research again. He had his first lab readings in one week. The first portion of his work depended on two methods. The first method employed a memristor – a memory chip suitable for both computing and faster, denser memory. He overlaid a semiconductor with 5hmC and, using existing semiconductor technology, was able to measure the results and compare the readings in terms of electrical signal variation and memory capacity. He owed this technique to HP (Hewlett-Packard), which had pioneered the first memristor and made it consumer friendly.

Daniel's second method was to coat a silicon memristor with a thin film of 5hmC and then to study what was going on inside. He found that this new device not only appeared to behave like flash memory, as first discovered by Dr. Anthony Kenyon at the University College of London, but also showed an embedded corrective intelligence. Flash memory devices, which switched gates On and Off at ten thousand nanoseconds (billionths of a second), had been around for forty-five years, but the biggest shocker was that memristors had a "remembering" quality and seemed unaffected when overloaded with complex commands: even when power was turned off, every bit of programmed instructions and memory was retained.

Researchers had tried to develop brain prostheses before, but with terrible results. Back in 2016 the challenge had been that natural signals emitted by the brain, had erratic voltage readings and were very hard to predict and mimic on an artificial opposite signal to communicate with. The closest success had been at the University of Southern California in Los Angeles. Dr. Theodore Burgen, who led the experimentation efforts, had had mild success in communicating to the hippocampus, the lower part of the brain from a microchip planted within the brain itself after studying and modeling the millions of electrical signals on his so called 'brain-chip'. He had provoked an outcry from fellow researchers, however, because he was tampering with an area of the brain that supposedly affects mood, awareness, consciousness, and memory—qualities directly linked to a person's identity.

The hippocampus is believed to "encode" experiences so they can be stored as long-term memories in another part of the brain. Dr. Burgen claimed that, because the hippocampus can be seen as a series of similar circuits that work in parallel, it should be possible to bypass the area if it were damaged. His results were inconclusive, however, because his patients did not consistently show improvements, and in some cases their deaths were actually accelerated.

The excitement was difficult to hide. Friends and colleagues on RadGio contacted Daniel, who would reply politely and broadcast reports of his tedious work, his hectic schedule, and his hope that he was working on something good for humanity. He teased his parents with the possibility of an impending breakthrough. RadGio, which had been created approximately twenty years earlier as a public service giving all people the opportunity to advertise on the radio, had mushroomed into a large social network. Much like a 24-7 targeted advertisement network, people used their individual RadGio stations to trade goods and services worldwide. It combined the phenomena of Facebook, YouTube, craigslist, and eBay into a single platform.

After reading numerous weekly reports, Dr. Lee realized that Daniel was onto that "something" he had promised. Toward the end of week eight, Daniel was studying every part of the human brain on the Department central lab data that were posted and linked to the various research centers worldwide, making an electronic interactive formulas, logging the many voltages he read on his simulator, and making sense of the information to devise a mathematical model of the right and left cortices, as well as the hippocampus. He then programmed his model on a biochip, which he wanted to attach to a patient's skull rather than implanting it in the brain. The biochip would then communicate with the brain via nanowires or electrodes placed on top of the damaged brain area known as "attitude." Power supply was an issue, but for now he was able, at least on his model, to record the electrical activity coming from the rest of the brain and to send the necessary instructions back to the simulated brain.

Dr. Lee visited Daniel at about 11 p.m., a relatively common work time for the few students in the field. Biophysicists seemed to have the will to stay away from the cafés scattered on University Avenue and the lure of marijuana smoke, which had become especially strong after the town redesigned its busiest six-block area and prohibited cars in the area after 7 p.m. Daniel paid no notice to the professor, who hovered around the new nuclear anaerobic equipment and incubators scattered around the entire wing of the second floor.

"What's up?" said Dr. Lee.

"Oh, hi, Doc. I'm getting there," Daniel said. "As a matter of fact, I have something very important to ask you. I'm staring my second phase. What if I add 5hmC to a DNA sequence whose specific function is known, coat the combination on a silicon memristor, charge it, and wire it straight to patients?"

"You mean, to their brains?" asked Dr. Lee.

"Yes. Let's call this chip Titan—self-describing, don't you think?"

"Yes. Keep going."

"We can use the old implant sensor method and stick the chip to a particular underperforming area in the brain. We can then translate the electric signals coming from that area to command functions on the Titan, like a neural interface making connections simulating neuron subtle energy flashes. And it will respond, Doc, I think it will."

Dr. Lee, intrigued, calmly responded, "That attitude in the brain is almost gone, dead—I mean, mute—in some patients. Where do you propose to get your power, young man?" Daniel did not hesitate. "Remember what you and Dr. Mathieson are famous for? Well, what do you say?"

Dr. Lee, beginning to appear amused, said, "Are you going to finish your idea?"

"Sorry, Doc, I am overly excited, and I have played out this hitch in my head and on my Phonepad so many thousands of times that it has become obvious to me. Using your method of generating actuators for our nanodevice, we can generate enough power for Titan to zap the brain in the exact area we want it. And as a backup plan, Doc, if you recall, Dr. Mathieson pioneered a photovoltaic implant that is successfully generating power wirelessly, sending infrared beams straight to the retinal chip for people to see every day. We can do the same. So, now, is it his method or yours that you want me to test?"

With a grin, Dr. Lee said, "Mine is better. You move, you get power, you stay healthy. Let's go for a drink on the avenue, smarty pants."

It was not unusual for a professor to go in town with a student. At Café Barron, Daniel felt comfortable enough to talk freely, speculating about what a scientific achievement his experiments would be if they were successful. After a couple glasses of Pinot Grigio, the question on the table was to imagine what would happen if Daniel's innovation improved the brain so much that a disabled person could turn into an athlete, or an autistic person could become socially normal. Patients would start writing about their transformations, they guessed.

Finishing his drink, Daniel toyed with another idea: "What if the 'fixed' patients can think better than us? What if they have a greater capacity to analyze, Doc?"

A blank look formed on Dr. Lee's face. He gazed past Daniel toward a flat, pastel yellow wall at the back of the café. "You never know, young man. Wow, that would be something, wouldn't it?" Then he regained his composure and, asserting his intellectual superiority, replied, "Well, before you can tap in to humans you need to follow university rules — and the law."

Daniel had thought of that as well. "I intend to put in a request for lab animals, and I'll need your signature," he replied. "I might ask for a primate. What do you think, Doc?"

Kindly but firmly, Dr. Lee suggested that Daniel work with small animals instead. Any type of monkey brought to the lab would require special handling, he pointed out, in addition to the exorbitant cost of approximately one million G just for the animal. Dr. Lee could not justify such an expenditure until Daniel had more concrete evidence to show. Lab animals had been controversial for at least eighty years. Opposition had become increasingly vocal, despite the recent U.S Supreme Court ruling that had made clear distinctions between the lives of humans and other animals. The majority opinion even stated that primates were animals and could be used for testing as long as the procedures were "humane and beneficial to the human race," as articulated by Justice Ryan Ballou, the youngest of the esteemed judges.

Daniel had no choice but to agree with his professor. He picked up the tab at Café Barron and zapped the bill on his PayGeo account, a mobile cash service usually residing on smart devices. After an uncomfortable silence, Daniel and Dr. Lee went their separate ways.

Dr. Lee's mind was spinning in many directions. He looked ahead as he walked but saw no one. He seemed burdened with the possibility that the experiment would get out of hand, but he could not put his finger on why. "Daniel is following all procedures," he thought. "He has been forthcoming about his progress and has shown great skills of deduction. . . . Dangerously optimistic, that's it! That's what's been bothering me. Daniel has been dangerously optimistic, though I cannot say I blame him."

Sipping a strong double espresso, Daniel strolled back to his lab. A few days later, he received a load of mice and rats for his experiment, a sign that Dr. Lee had not forgotten about him. Daniel was ready to roll up his sleeves and begin the second phase of this daunting experiment.

He needed to begin with a process called phenotype, or the study of animals via their observable physical or biochemical characteristics—such as shape, color, and movement—as determined by both genetic makeup and environmental influences. He would also need to do a genotype of his animal subjects—a study of their actual genetic material. The distinction between genotype and phenotype studies was crucial in Daniel's study.

Daniel had to create an undisputed methodology that would survive future scrutiny and be free of any margin of error. He needed to apply the 5hmC from each mutation, derived from a well-known area in the brain, to a silicon memristor with definitive knowledge of premutation function and let it self-assemble on the Titan.

Daniel had chosen to work on mice. The advantage here was that scientists had already identified spontaneous mutations on all mouse genes. Daniel would subject the creatures to radiation or chemical mutagenesis, causing the mice to mimic specific dysfunctions in well-mapped areas of their brains. He would use this approach at a fast pace with mouse strains that had been shown to display a certain phenotype and had been bred selectively for a given behavioral trait. Another method, called forward genetics, was known to provide very unusual animal models; however, the genetic basis of the abnormal behavior was often obscure. Given that limitation, Daniel required that the sites of the mutations in the brain be mapped and sequenced before and after radiation treatments. A laborious and time-consuming process in the past, the mapping and sequencing now could be done in a matter of days with modern nuclear equipment. Daniel would use the classical method of reverse genetics, to fend off critics and hopefully to get the same results he had gathered on other experiments. Reverse genetics is an old type of analysis that precedes genotype and phenotype. Here, a specific gene is targeted for disruption or modification, and the mutants are evaluated for behavioral abnormalities. In the gene-targeting approach, which was very popular in the early part of 2030 decade, reduction in gene expression (expressed in the protein they encode) in vivo is accomplished through the introduction of RNA interference (RNA are the none coding protein genes) that targets a specific RNA species. Although this approach does not completely suppress all expression (behaviors) of the target gene, it can reduce it to 98 percent, a level sufficient to produce quantifiable biochemical and behavioral changes yielding excellent results.

Behavioral assessment in mice and rats had come a long way as well. The past century had witnessed advances in behavioral phenotype. These important steps had shown that animal test subjects should first be checked for general health, reflexive and motor capabilities, emotionality, anxiety, affective and social behaviors, consummator responses (like eating and drinking), and learning and memory. Partially due to the use of mutant mice, the past decade had witnessed numerous advances in identification of molecular mechanisms that underlie a wide variety of behaviors in animals. Daniel could tap in to work by investigators who had produced many strains of mutations with 5hmC in order to examine the roles of different genes in cognitive behavior. Daniel himself had isolated N-methyl-D-aspartate (NMDA), a receptor that had been shown to play an important role in hippocampal activities (the hippocampus is the part of the brain that is involved in memory formation, organization, and storage), to use for coating his memristor over a 5hmC silicon memristor. This, he noticed, created an incredible potentiation (the long-lasting enhancement in signal transmission between two neurons); he was able to encode 5hmC with a particular task and thus allow great retention of memory and learning. At the same time, however, he discovered that any disruption in the gene code NR1, or even in part of a protein involved in passing signals between neurons, was potentially lethal.

During his eighth week, Daniel discovered that mice with targeted disruption of a gene in the brain CA1 region of the hippocampus survived but showed severe impairment in spatial learning and memory. To deal with this delicate task, he designed a broad series of tests that were administered to all mice. He used various power supplies on the 5hmC silicon memristors. These tedious tests of sensory and motor function, neurophysiological status, and emotionality would take eight long months to show results.

Since many tests of cognitive performance in mice relied upon vision, it was important for Daniel to conduct a detailed neurophysiological examination of vision to determine whether the mice with the added 5hmC silicon memristors responded to light differently compared with others, whether they had the same depth perception, and whether they had the advantage of discriminating patterned simulations (linking behaviors to certain animal patterns). First he evaluated and compared pupillary responses to light. He would hold the mice by hand and shine a penlight into their eyes for three- and five-second intervals over many trials. He filmed the mice with a special ultra resolution 3-D digitized camera, spent countless evenings analyzing frame by frame each animal's response to the various memristors, and painstakingly chose the correct brain area to tap his nanowire on. He made sure to test all types of mice, including wild type (WT) and knockout (KO) type born in labs. Next, he tested responses to light and dark by placing the mice in a passive-avoidance apparatus. Within a few weeks, he concluded that there were no genotype differences in the latency for the mice to leave a lighted compartment and enter a darkened chamber, or in the time spent in each of the chambers. This was a sign of emotional and neurophysiologic resiliency. These data suggested that all genotypes with or without 5hmC silicon memristors could discriminate light from dark and that the various animals' levels of emotionality were similar.

Daniel then examined depth perception by slowly lowering the different mice toward a bench. WT and KO mice with and without the 5hmC extended their forepaws upon being lowered to the lab bench at different heights, and then he tested whether the mice could track a moving object within the visual field. Here the results were astonishing: mice wired with Titan would retain countless mazes in upward of a hundred configurations and would remember the escape route in every instance, while the rest could muster the memory of only one or two. As no genotype differences were discerned in any of the vision tests, Daniel concluded that the mice with the 5hmC silicon memristors had huge advantages due to various mutations, including enhanced memory capacity.

Keeping the pressure on Dr. Lee, Daniel again requested a primate so that he could show more elaborate results. Dr. Lee put in a request to Stanford's medical procurement office to buy such animal from a company called Humane Kenya, but his request required authorization from the head of procurements due to the high cost, estimated to be close to 8,000G plus shipping from Africa. Dr. Lee would make a weekly call to the procurement office, as he was being given all sorts of excuses for not providing the animal—"We're waiting on the budget," "We still have to put it on the meeting agenda," "The PO will issue next cycle," and so on. Dr. Lee even went as far as attempting to borrow a primate from the University of San Francisco through an old colleague, anthropology department head Dr. William Browder. Dr. Browder knew the head of purchases for USF's lab but could spare only rabbits or pigs for his friend; primates were too valuable to part with, even temporarily and for nonintrusive trials.

Daniel kept in touch with Mirvet sporadically. She was able to RadGio him few times; he kept tabs on her station and from time to time would write her a note or comment on a broadcast she had made. Mirvet had wanted to see Daniel after his accident but had been unable to leave her job; besides, Daniel had returned to the United States within a few short days. She had initiated the contact by sending him a short, polite note: "Hope you feel better. Hope to see you in Egypt next summer." He had been overjoyed to receive the note and could barely control his emotion as he fought the urge to tell her that he had been running after her the evening he was stabbed. His reply was also polite: "Thank you. Keep tuning in to my RadGio, and wish me luck."

Daniel continued to wonder if Mirvet knew more than she was letting on. She definitely should have guessed that he had been after her on that fateful evening, that he had wanted to say good-bye before leaving the following day. He could tell that Mirvet had a soft spot for him. But then, being of a different culture and living on the opposite side of the earth, she probably did not trust either her feelings or his. And Daniel was right—she had even been impressed by the shyness that he'd displayed when she was around—but it was he who needed to make the first move. In a Middle Eastern culture, it remained improper for a woman to show emotion to the opposite sex first. Mirvet had been very disappointed that Daniel had never spoken to her in private—and the moment he had tried, he had been stabbed. Maybe now, she reasoned, she could carry on a heart-to-heart conversation with him.

Daniel would "bee" (broadcast) to Mirvet's signal regularly. This time he asked what had happened to the kids at the rug factory and whether the disabled were treated medically in any way. She replied that all was the same, and nothing moved quickly in her part of the world. When they chatted on closed-broadcast circuit (CBC), Daniel asked Mirvet to find out Egypt's requirements for performing a trial medical procedure. Daniel had the resources to find all the answers from the comfort of his apartment or lab, but he remained intrigued by Mirvet and had found a good reason to keep in touch. She was delighted.

Egypt had plenty of laws on the books, and referring the new 2024 constitution, which had a heavy British influence, Mirvet joked that her lawyer friends told her, "Animals have better rights than humans in Egypt." One evening Mirvet sent Daniel a CBC that she had spoken to the parents of one of the disabled girls at the rug factory, and her parents had agreed to a treatment that would be kept secret from authorities. It was a legal borderline case, as parents of a minor were the only arbiter on treatment of their kids. And for an experimental procedure, the law required a certification from a medical doctor or institution to the effect that the administered treatment was a "medical trial method [that] may lead to a cure, that has no negative effects on patient, and that is reversible and humane."

These criteria were difficult to meet, especially the reversible part. While experimenting on mice, Daniel had found that a mistake in targeting the wrong area of the brain with infrared low laser circuit could be lethal; surprisingly, the mice had experienced a better recovery when he had used a nanowire intrusion instead. But that technique required a supervised surgical procedure in a hospital setting. As their chat went back and forth, Daniel suggested that if he could get the required letter from Stanford, a renowned university hospital, it would certainly suffice. Daniel began doubting himself; he was torn between his quest to conquer a diseased brain and to prove his superior method, thus bringing cognitive and motor improvement to the disabled children, and the grave risk to the same people he was trying to help. There would be a serious or deadly outcome if he missed the mark. He had no immediate solution to this old ethical question, and he could not guarantee that a letter from Stanford would even satisfy the Egyptian law.

For days Daniel thought about whether he should tell Dr. Lee about Mirvet and the progress of finding a candidate for his new procedure in Asyut. Finally, one afternoon, he decided to test the waters. He sent his latest progress report and rushed to the professor's office. When he arrived, Daniel was short of breath—a good way to hide his anxiety. He began by telling Dr. Lee that a friend who lived in Cairo had suggested Daniel do his testing there. He told the professor that Egypt's laws seemed more relaxed than American ones, and experimental medical testing involved far less red tape there than anywhere else.

Dr. Lee was surprised. He told Daniel that he had no doubt that Egypt was a signatory to the Medical Research and Development Treaty (MRDT), which was closely affiliated with the World Health Organization. This treaty had been signed back in 2011, when he was a student at UC Berkeley. Dr. Lee did concede that laws in some of the signatory countries didn't mean much, and that he had no doubt that a lot of cruel and black-market testing still went on, just as it had in China in the previous century. Daniel commented that it would be a real pity if he could help humankind but was unable to cut through red tape while people continued to suffer.

Dr. Lee had come to know his student well and had grown increasingly impressed with Daniel's intelligence and creativity. He realized that although Daniel was academically accomplished, he was very impatient and had an adventurous side that might get out of hand if left unchecked. Dr. Lee reminded Daniel to provide a little bit more details on his weekly progress reports — anything related to the Titan project, as it was now called. And "anything" meant communications with anyone relating to the Titan.

"Is this requirement legal?" joked Daniel.

"Yes," Dr. Lee replied. "You are young, and the worst part is that you are very smart — that's where the danger lies. When the time comes, I will help you put in an application with the MRDT. I know people there. We can follow up with them, and within, oh, less than a year, you can take your published paper and results out in the open, and everyone will welcome you — including the people in

Egypt. Therefore, please concentrate on getting correct results, and don't rush to save the disabled yet. The world has been waiting for ages; it can wait some more."

Dr. Lee had gauged Daniel correctly, but his student had one other quality that was below the professor's radar: ambition. On the surface, ambition seemed to be an honorable trait; Daniel had been born with a fire in his belly and had watched his parents become achievers in their fields, and he had a sense of respect for folks who worked their way up from the bottom. To him, ambition was entangled with fame, which was a product of success. He could relate to fame in the narrow scientific, biomedical, and possibly astrophysics sense. He relished new discoveries and knew that he was as capable as anyone in his field. On the other hand, he had no tolerance for fame in terms of modern singers, dancers, or even actors. He had a mild patience for the classical eighteenth- and nineteenth-century composers, as he had watched his father mesmerized by Mendelssohn and Beethoven while growing up.

Even as a kid, Daniel knew that ambition could be dangerous. He had watched cartoons that featured smart but evil guys who wanted to take planet Earth hostage. In the end a strong, decent human would save the day. That would be Daniel, and now it was he who would be famous. He would be credited with carrying out God's plan to cure the masses right from his lab.

Mirvet called Daniel one afternoon at about 3 p.m., when he was in his lab. He was very surprised to hear from her, particularly because it was 1 a.m. in Egypt. He asked if there was an urgent matter, made sure she was safe, and, finally revealing some emotion, told her that he missed her. Mirvet took notice, and she glimpsed a different person in him, someone compassionate and loving, though still shy. She replied that a man named Adel, the father of Sara, the little disabled girl at the museum, had instructed Mirvet to tell Daniel that Adel would be willing to risk "all he's got" — including money — for Daniel to administer his new "drug" to Sara. Apparently Mirvet had not gone into much detail with Adel; she had promoted Daniel's work as a new drug he was in the process of discovering, rather than as an invasive procedure.

Daniel asked if Sara's father or mother could speak any English so that he could communicate with them. Mirvet answered that Sara's mother was not around, but Mirvet herself could translate for Adel, who was right next to her and could be heard yelling, "Daniel, Daniel!" helbbbb (help). Mirvet apologized for the chaos. Daniel pointed out that it might be illegal for him to do anything to help Sara, and he asked Mirvet to explain that his procedure was dangerous and might even kill the girl.

Mirvet paused. Then Daniel could hear her translation, followed by Adel saying, "Kweyess, kweyess . . ." ("Understood . . ."). Mirvet finally said to Daniel, "Can you come over?"

Daniel's heart melted, and the thought of seeing Mirvet in flesh and blood, after about a year of chatting with her and seeing her on his folding Phonepad, made him blush. After some hesitation, he said, "Sure."

"When can you come?" she asked.

"Well, I have to finish writing my paper, get my professor to sign off on my work, and . . . oh, I really don't know."

Daniel let Mirvet in on some basic details of his procedure. He said he believed it could help humans but had yet to receive even one monkey to help him complete his dissertation. Occasionally Mirvet would interrupt Daniel and explain to Adel a few highlights, especially the part about the monkey, Adel could be heard repeating, "Ehna kollena khelet Allah" ("We are all God's creatures"). Daniel heard this a half dozen times before he ended the call.

This was the first time Daniel had spoken to Mirvet at length; the call went on for over an hour. Daniel brought up the legal issues associated with experimental testing—how it was punishable with a fine and imprisonment, and how the United Nations had an international treaty designed to clamp down on using humans as guinea pigs, especially in the developed world. He went on to explain that these laws in the UN treaty had been established late in the previous century, when organ harvesting had been prevalent in China and South Asia. Daniel's words kept falling on deaf ears, however. Before he and Mirvet said good-bye, Adel asked Mirvet to translate one more thing: "Sara is dying anyway."

After bidding Mirvet farewell with a sparkle in his eyes and a promise to stay in touch, Daniel found himself extremely moved by the call. He felt the need to do something in a hurry. He figured he could conclude his paper and submit it to the patent office within weeks. He knew there would be more twists and turns as Titan embarked on an uncharted course.

Daniel needed Dr. Lee's consent to wind down. He was excused from being a teaching assistant at the moment, as he had put in the time during his master's program. Thanks to a grant from the National Institutes of Health (NIH), coupled with Stanford's own endowment, it had been possible to fund his research thus far. Publishing his dissertation was another condition for attaining his PhD. Daniel had compiled a fantastic collection of narratives detailing his experiments and had written an impressive volume encompassing the entire study. It came as no surprise when he asked Dr. Lee if he could "check out" (graduate) a year and a half after the Titan project had been launched, which would be a remarkable achievement. Dr. Lee accepted Daniel's dissertation and asked him to take an oral exam with four microbiology professors and one microphysics professor. In the meantime, Daniel and Dr. Lee reviewed the patent application that the university staff council had put together. Dr. Lee suggested that his own name as co inventor be removed, as he realized that Daniel Oakley was fully responsible for all three criteria for the granting of a patent: the novelty, the inventive step, and the industrial application.

Daniel was appreciative of this gesture but did not understand it. He knew that Stanford would be guaranteed a certain percentage of any monetary rewards from industry use. But there remained a potentially huge direct economic benefit to Dr. Lee, who had helped keep Daniel focused and had demanded additional data that had shaped the Titan project. It seemed that Dr. Lee had reached a point in his life where fame had become a burden, and he planned to retire and lie low before long. His cousin Justin Wu, an orthopedist working in the military, had promised to keep Dr. Lee's mind active with a part-time consultant job with decent pay.

Finally, the day came. The professors sat at a conference table on the fifth floor in the Fairchild Building. Daniel appeared with his Phonepad, a powerful, pocket-size instrument that could fold into two or three screens. Phonepads, which had taken off about ten years earlier, combined the so-called smartphones of the past with laptop and desktop computers. Their speed and memory were unmatched. They could carry not only money, but also a person's entire wealth in terms of owned traded commodities on the different stock exchanges throughout the world, proof of ownership of every conceivable item, including real estate. Made more famous with the introduction of the "poison pill" by Intel, a disabling command that could be activated by users either permanently or temporarily if a Phonepad were lost or stolen. All this was possible due to PayGeo cloud computing or other similar cloud carriers. Daniel was able to present his entire project by unfolding his three screens and projecting onto the wall his entire technical architectures, his experimentation approach, and the phases leading up to results, all with voice-recognition prompts.

Dr. Salwan began with a statement rather than a question: "So, you filed a patent, Daniel."

"Yes, sir," Daniel replied.

"Why?"

"Well, Why not, patents as we know them began in the republic of Venice in 1474. Don't believe the Brits and the story of King Henry VI—he was a partner with the glass merchant."

The room erupted in a loud laugh that was atypical of cultured professors in esteemed halls. Daniel was referring to when King Henry VI allowed a merchant who had invented a method of coloring glass to do exclusive business in his realm for twenty years. A new study suggested that the king had profited from the scheme. In truth, the republic of Venice had issued the first protection of new ideas, with a limit of two years.

Daniel had won the professors' hearts immediately; now he needed to win their minds.

Dr. Salwan continued, "So, why do you call it Titan?"

"Well, Titan was the god of knowledge in Greek mythology, and I think my silicon memristor is full of knowledge. . . ."

What ensued was a five-hour questioning and examination of Daniel's mind—his modus operandi, the reasoning behind each experiment, and comparisons of similar tests yielding similar or different results depending on conditions and methodologies. During this time the panel's refreshments consisted only of water. The professors were clearly intrigued by Daniel's answers and impressed with his dissertation. Dr. Lee asked some questions whose answers he already knew, just to show off his student prodigy.

There was an objection by Dr. Nueyen that Daniel's dissertation was unfinished. Daniel would need to test his invention on primates before he could declare victory and ask for approval to use on humans. Daniel knew precisely what she meant, but he argued that the primate would not be forthcoming for another year. "Besides," he said, "Once results are confirmed, my work will still be unfinished. Human testing is the key, and it could take years to get the FDA's approval." Daniel then requested to continue working for Dr. Lee, with or without pay, while he contemplated his next career move, so that he could try to build and reconfirm his findings.

The last word came from Dr. Bdair: "I like what I see, and knowing Dr. Lee, I believe he will not object to your lab work, assuming you don't disrupt anyone else's."

Dr, Lee smiled in agreement. "Yes, of course."

Dr. Bdair continued. "Watching you talk about Titan — the crisp details and your thought process — is very refreshing indeed. I think this institution has again proved its worth by bringing a talent like yours to fruition, as it has done for more than a century and half. Please remember, however, that the ends don't justify the means. You have a long way ahead of you, son."

The voting came next. All the professors gave Daniel the nod.

Daniel called home and asked his mom if he could still stay in the downstairs bedroom. "Of course, son," she said. "We would be delighted. What happened? Did you run out of money?"

"No, Mom, it's not about money. I'm done. My project was approved!"

"Oh, my lord, you were supposed to be in for another two years—your dad budgeted for that! This is the best news I've heard in a long time. You're sure it's not about money?"

"Please, Mom, no. But you can call me doctor if you want. I even have a patent in the works."

"Oh, my lord, that's wonderful. Your dad will fall out of his chair—I wish you could be here to see it. Sorry, but I can't wait to tell him. I'll tell you what he does."

Although Daniel's parents knew the basic outline of the project he was working on, the details were Greek to them. They tried hard to remember what he had said during dinners at home or on their family trip to Egypt, but they could not pinpoint any of the ideas or make sense of the difficult lexicon he used. They were pleased that he had essentially finished his PhD within a year and half at a world-renowned school, a truly impressive feat. His father thought of the jobs Daniel could have and wondered what the pay would be. But first thing was first: the Oakleys needed to throw Daniel a party. His mother wanted him to start mingling with the opposite sex.

Meanwhile, Daniel wanted to focus on next steps. He was offered an associate professorship at Stanford, but he gently asked for some time to think about it. He also received offers from the military (perhaps due to Dr. Lee's connection),

Genentech, and a pharmaceutical firm in Rome. He went home that evening but did not tell his parents much more; he was exhausted and in need of a good rest.

Chapter 4

An "Invitation" from the Feds

Daniel had barely had a good night's sleep in two years. He could not rest. Too many variables were undefined in his head: his life path, his work, his new idea, and even his social world seemed to be up in the air. The most troubling factors, however, were his Titan project and the results of his experiments. He played out all sorts of scenarios in his head, from success to downright failure. He would fall asleep thinking about perfecting one method while double-checking another.

Daniel had the gift of thinking outside the box; even before embarking on Titan, he had known that he was destined to find something others had overlooked and to make a discovery that would help humanity. He had an air of mild arrogance, and even as a child he had been known not to repeat himself. He believed that he deserved a spot with the "great ones," and he had set out to earn it. He had grown up recognizing that intelligence alone was not enough; he needed to match it with hard work.

In addition, Daniel was careful not to let his emotions dictate his behaviors: he did not squander valuable time with the opposite sex, and he had avoided wild environments with drugs and alcohol. He was known to show up at parties, show his face and pretend to be part of the crowd, but then quickly depart as he offered one of a large dictionary of excuses that somehow remained original in his mind. His only serious girlfriend had been an Irishwoman named Niamph, a student visitor taking a course for undergraduate seniors majoring in biophysics. She had done the trick of stimulating Daniel's mind (among other things) by indulging him with debates on stem cell research and electrodes. He had been taken by her intelligence and simplicity and had felt great pain when the time had come for her to go back to Dublin. They were both ambitious and had unfinished business ahead of them, so romance was not going to change any of their plans. Daniel and Niamph stayed in contact but slowly grew apart.

Daniel would often tell his parents that there was a lot to do and see in the world before getting tied down by marriage and a family. He joked that there was not enough daylight and wished humans could work a lot more. He felt there was no need to sleep the six to eight hours recommended by doctors, and there would one day be a pill to give humans just one hour of deep sleep providing sufficient rest for the twenty-three remaining hours of the day. Daniel loved what he was doing, and it showed. All along he had known what he wanted. Even as a child, he had planned out his destiny by himself, apparently without any role model. He seemed to have the willpower to face the many tribulations of life.

That Sunday morning, Daniel received an email from the United States Patent and Trademark Office (USPTO). The message, which was sent with a carbon copy to his lawyer, directed Daniel to get in touch with the office by Monday at 8 a.m. PST for an interview by an examiner named John Weinstock. It included an address that Daniel could use to access a videoconference.

Daniel was surprised that the USPTO office was open on a Sunday, but he presumed the workload had required some examiners to work overtime, or perhaps email deliveries had been programmed to go on a weekend. He wondered why Samuel Kasedy, Stanford University's chief patent attorney, had said he would not hear from anyone for over a year. It had been only twelve weeks from the date of his application. Daniel assumed that great improvements had been made in D.C. — at least something was working well in the capital. Either way, he would find out soon; Mr. Kasedy would be at the conference.

Being an early riser, Daniel prepared all his documents and findings, reviewed his materials, and got set up for the videoconference in his spacious bedroom downstairs. He had thought about calling Mr. Kasedy, just in case it would be advisable to avoid any particular subjects that may be irrelevant, but he had not wanted to bother the lawyer on a Sunday or an early Monday morning. Besides, Daniel had nothing to fear or rescind. It was the opposite: he was prepared to add evidence that the patent office didn't know yet. He was thinking of a benign way to run his test on humans, and he wanted to check with the FDA on ways to go about it.

Daniel unwound two of his Phonepad screens and connected to the conference. He was surprised to see that there were three people present on the other side — and Mr. Kasedy was not one of them. Likening the call to a trial, Daniel joked that he would need his counsel in order to proceed, but the gentlemen on the opposite side could see through his mock seriousness. They introduced themselves as Mr. John Weinstock, Mr. Browder Sigmund, and Dr. Justin Wu — Dr. Lee's relative and head of the regenerative medicine department. After a short pause, Mr. Weinstock told Daniel that his counsel, Mr. Kasedy, would not be joining the conference. They had relayed to Mr. Kasedy that this meeting would not be technical in nature; rather, the government would be stating a position accompanied by an employment offer that Daniel's attorney could choose to review with his client at a later time.

Daniel, overcome with joy but intimidated, looked at his screens and wondered what he should do.

"Is this a job offer?" he asked.

Dr. Wu said, "Sort of. We need you to listen carefully, please. Your patent application has been deemed to be of national interest, and thus it must be kept secret. Even after multiple examinations, we cannot publish it. Mr. Oakley, your patent is likely to be granted, but it will stay out of the public's eyes – again, for national security reasons."

Daniel opened his brown eyes wide, moved his Phonepad closer, and said, "Are you serious? Is this a movie script?"

Dr. Wu continued. "Not to bore you with details, but ever since March of 2012, the government has either prevented the public issuance of many patents or, as in your case, issued the patents in secret. We understand that this practice is new to you. Now, it is to your credit that we believe your Titan will likely achieve one or more patents. It's just that we believe your invention is extremely dangerous to be out in the marketplace at this point."

Daniel asked, "Who is 'we'?"

"The government," Mr. Browder replied.

Mr. Weinstock continued. "There is no doubt in my mind that if the findings on your application are correct, yours would be one of the best inventions that made it onto my desk. My compliments."

Dr. Wu explained, "While the government may take a secret patent for its own use, the patent holder retains all rights to it and may manufacture and sell it on the open market after a period of time that will be determined by our office. It can take three, five, ten years; in your case, we just don't know yet. And, by the way, the patent remains in force against all other parties. If you disagree with our decision to keep the patent secret, you, as patent owner, would have the right to take action against the United States in a special court called the U.S. Court of Federal Claims. There, you may recover reasonable compensation for the use of the patent, if it's been used. Mind you, we can't tell you if the government intends to manufacture Titan, or even to contract with someone else to make it. A decision like that is taken higher up the ladder — maybe even the top."

Dr. Wu smiled and continued. "Although usually the first instinct of the inventor is to go to the court I mentioned, I have done this many times and have seen it all. You needn't bother yourself at this stage, as you would not have a case. Again, the government has the right to make this decision, believe me, and besides, this court usually hinges its decisions on issues of patent infringement rather than challenges to the validity of the government's secrecy requirement. The court is famous for setting royalty figures, but without the patented goods there are no figures, and without figures there are no royalties."

Daniel responded, "This is way too much for me, gentlemen."
"Relax Daniel, relax" Mr. Browder said.
"So," Dr. Wu said, "what we are doing here is preempting all these issues and making you an offer to come work with us. You may hire an attorney at a later point, when the patent is granted. If the government were to decide to produce anything, your counsel could help you negotiate your royalty, through licensing to the government.

"As of now, it is unlikely that an actual Titan, as you call it, would be made to generate income. Be prepared that it might remain theoretical and untested. But considering the claims you are making, the Titan is akin to a powerful weapon.

Daniel said, "I don't understand how you read weapons, or even an insinuation of negative use, in my application. As I pointed out, this invention would help the disabled, don't you think?"

"Well, you can cook with a kitchen knife, but you can kill with it too. I am sorry; I can't explain it now," said Dr. Wu.

Daniel got up and asked to end the meeting. Checking his temper, he said, "I definitely need counsel on these matters. I need to go now."

Mr. Weinstock smiled and said, "We are not worried about what Titan will do to the disabled; it's everyone else they are worried about."

Before Daniel could sign off, Dr. Wu raised his voice and said, "Don't you want to hear our offer?"

"What is it?" asked Daniel.

"You would be coming to Livermore Lab, not far from where you are, and you would be making half a million G the first year. And, you just might be seeing Dr. Lee there."
Daniel reiterated that he needed to think about the offer without any pressure for at least two weeks.

"Shoot for one week, please," Dr. Wu said.

Daniel called Samuel Kasedy a few times before he got a reply. He asked if Samuel had received an invitation to be on the call this morning.

"Yes," Samuel admitted, and proceeded to tell Daniel that in his many years of experience, he had not seen anything like this — although he had heard of it. Samuel had received a call from Dr. Wu in addition to the initial email message from the patent office. Dr. Wu had told Samuel in the politest terms that he would not be welcome at the videoconference, which involved an employment offer rather than the technical details of a patent. Dr. Wu also had promised not to prejudice the patent in any way.

"Dr. Wu hardly spoke about the patent in the technical way," Samuel reported to Daniel. "He likened it to a weapon patent that the government needed to control. You call that 'without prejudice'? From what I know, this type of fight with the government is unwinnable in most cases. It may be in your best interest to attempt to negotiate a license with them before they take the entire patent, by hook or by crook. Such negotiations may establish an acceptable royalty rate for you."

"But they might never make Titan," Daniel said.

"Well, I can recommend an attorney who will convince them otherwise," Samuel responded. "His name is John Massetti. To explain a bit further, the government may put restrictions on a patent, in narrative language that you can agree with. For example, your patent could stipulate that Titan may be used only on patients who need it for specific reasons. From now on, we must focus on making a case that the invention is viable, propitious, and necessary. That is my opinion for now, but we'll check with John. I am sorry this is happening, Daniel. If it's any consolation, I suppose it's a price that overachievers and intelligent folks pay now and then. The main thing is not to panic; stay calm and look at this as an opportunity. I am going to call John. He's well experienced in fighting patent takeover by the government. Give me time to reach him and explain, and then call him within an hour or so."

Daniel began to research precedents. Within a few hours he had read volumes of repetitive materials, some dating to 1948 or 2006. He found out that eminent domain powers allowed federal and local governments to buy property or to take other actions in the name of the public good. The idea of just compensation for the exercise of eminent domain was even written into the U.S. Constitution. While it often had been applied to real estate law — for example, to build roads after compensating landowners for the sale (coerced or otherwise) of their property — eminent domain had not been a common legal instrument in the health care business. Daniel's research led him to a 1948 eminent domain case in which the government gained access to patented nuclear physics processes, leading to the making of the atom bomb. Although the law required fair compensation, the idea was that the public should pay in some form for what it needed for the common good. Daniel read that economists had tried unsuccessfully to estimate the cost of taking a drug patent — the closest to a Titan patent — and to create a royalty compensation scale. However, the government always contested these cases in courts.

According to Daniel's sources, the government seldom exercised eminent domain, partly because of the weight of the free-enterprise tradition that honored patents and innovation in U.S. commerce.

John Massetti was an intelligent attorney. Ten years earlier, he had had a personal experience defending his own patent when he had filed an application for the Occio eye chip, which involved both software and hardware. The software was to be used on Phonepads and other portable devices, while the hardware consisted of an inexpensive, portable eye chip that could be dropped anywhere, helping to form an "Occioweb" of information that could be traded by users. This chip used a small amount of sun energy or heat; it essentially self-energized with no battery. Some were able to tackle commands or even mobility as in commanding Occioweb to move, hide or even fly. Access was granted to users in exchange for money or otherwise. The device used GPSX's newest satellite to hone in on the surrounding environment. It could detect whatever the user wanted — shapes, cars, trucks, boats, and so on — and could perform many tasks, including visual reconnaissance, elevation, temperature, and pressure, with or without permission. The government had deemed the patent military in nature and had contested its publishing, citing the device's potential use for spying. In the end, the invention was never disclosed to the public.

Sam talked to John, and they agreed on the proper course of action. Daniel called the lawyer soon afterward.

"Hello, Dr. Oakley," John said.

Daniel replied, "That doesn't sound right. Call me Daniel, please."

John asked if he could read the entire patent application, and Daniel agreed to send it. Then John asked Daniel to explain in bullet points what the invention was all about. Daniel stuck to the point and did not go through tedious details. John then briefly laid out his personal experience with the eye chip and his own lawsuit. He explained that his first task would be to study Titan thoroughly and get on the government's good side. He told Daniel that there was a legal precedent for such government patent takeover actions but that Daniel should not be alarmed.

John's second task would be to write a brief explaining how Daniel's patent was benign and did not constitute a national security in this case. In the meantime Daniel needed to visit John's office in person to sign an engagement letter and to discuss the fees associated with such an undertaking.

"What about the job offer at Livermore Lab?" Daniel asked.

"Well, that I cannot advise on now; my gut reaction is that these two issues should stay separate, and it may or may not be to your advantage to work for them. Ask if they can send you a detailed written offer for us to review."

Daniel did just that. He got in touch with his earlier callers from the patent office, asked them to send the detailed employment offer in its entirety, and requested thirty days to consider it. Dr. Wu agreed to send the offer within two days but asked that Daniel reply in two weeks.

For the next few days Daniel was distraught. He tried unsuccessfully to hide his anxiety from his family. Appearing disoriented and unable to focus, he conversed at the bare minimum. His father, Robert, began to worry that a mental illness had taken hold of his youngest son. With Ama's help he arranged for a psychiatrist friend, Ann, to come over for dinner. His wife guessed Robert's main purpose but was afraid even to contemplate the notion of something being wrong with her son. Still, Robert was not in the habit of inviting female friends to dinner.

When Ann arrived, Robert briefed her on his son's condition and behavior before having Daniel come upstairs. At dinner, Ann and her daughter Anaya conversed with Daniel. Although he seemed withdrawn and distant at times, he seemed as normal as people came. Anaya, who had gotten her medical degree at Stanford, was like a sister to Daniel. They had grown up together, and Daniel was very happy to see her. During the appetizers course, he opened up to Anaya: "I know I seem spaced out," he said, "but there is a lot on my mind. I cannot get used to having a lot of time on my hands. Being in academia for a long time makes you lose touch with the real world. I have a few job offers that I have not shared with anyone. Once I understand them myself, I will share them."

Daniel's loud confession to Anaya came as a great relief to Robert. It seemed Daniel wanted to put his parents at ease. He knew all about mental illness and the effect it has on a family — not to mention a patient. He felt bad that he was not answering his parents' polite questions, but he was pleased that the evening went well for everyone.

A gentle ring indicated that a message had come through Daniel's Phonepad. It was a twenty-six-page employment offer from Dr. Wu's office and needed to be signed by Friday the 14th. Daniel took note of a few glaring excerpts:

> If patent holder fails to comply with the disclosure provisions of the parties . . . this contract unambiguously provides that in such a case, the government may obtain title to the subject invention. . . . Any use of patent must be government authorized. . . . The government and its contractors are not required to pay reasonable compensation for patent if infringement occurs overseas.

To top it off, there was a complicated clause that involved "authorizations and consent laws," with an indemnity clause absolving the government from any liability.

Daniel knew enough to understand that he was being treated unfairly. The long hours he'd spent working on his invention, the complex experiments he had conducted, and the originality of his ideas would be handed on a silver platter to an entangled bureaucratic bazaar with no end in sight. He passed his employment contract on to John but surreptitiously made up his mind that regardless of the attorney's advice, even if he were to work at Livermore, he would not stay there long, and he would play by the government's rules only temporarily.

Daniel had grown up during the early days of the Jackson administration. He remembered his father being opposed to Jackson's policies, which he said were part of "the big government complex." Daniel was influenced greatly by his father and learned to love his country, admiring the Constitution and its balanced system of government, which countries around the world continued to emulate. He recalled his father telling him that there was no better country on

Earth, that the United States would outlast the Roman Empire by a magnitude of ten, and that the American genius lay in the inherent freedoms 'protected' by the Constitution: "all men are created equal," "inalienable rights," "endowed by God," and so on. Robert had told Daniel that these rights were not given by government, because whatever the government gave, it could take back, humans are born to be free.

The political dynamics of the Oakley family were low-key. Robert would complain about the process for securing a building permit; he claimed the application process took more time than the actual labor of building. He was an architect and an entrepreneur with little patience for unions and waste. He had a soft side as well, however. Daniel remembered Robert driving with the family in a Lincoln Navigator as they donated food to churches and soup kitchens around the mission districts and the poor neighborhoods of Hunters Point, by the bay.

Daniel read and understood the philosophical differences between what used to be called the liberal left and the conservative right, now called statist and constitutionalist. Where the latter did not believe in a "living and breathing" constitution that changed with modernity and lifestyle, they preferred that government stay small, that taxes be as low as possible, and that the underclass be given the bare minimum (on only a temporary basis) so that they would be enticed to work. On the other hand, statists didn't mind increasing regulations, raising taxes, and taking care of the weak and needy in society. To them, big government was essential to a society that did not necessarily know what was best for it. Daniel knew that both views, taken to their extremes, were unhealthy; one could create anarchy, while the other could lead to totalitarianism. Having supported either ideas at one time or another, he was truly in the middle.

Friday came too soon, and Daniel was faced with the dilemma that he had expected. The choices were limited. He could take no patent, solicit any commercial use, and ultimately make a profit. The government could legally obstruct patent proliferation and publication and take it from its rightful owner, as there were precedents that allowed such a move. He could fight the government in court, but it would be an exhausting and costly process that neither he nor anyone he knew could afford. He could work in Livermore, presumably on the same project, and make an above-average living, but he would be confined to a contract that would limit his freedom and take away his long-sought-after dream of fame and fortune.

John was not all negative; he offered a small window of hope. After talking to the government counsel he felt they had a bit of room to maneuver. At the federal court he could submit a brief articulating that Daniel's invention did not raise issues of national security, agreeing to restricted use in commerce and continuous reporting to the regenerative medicine department on the progress of testing and production of Titan, limiting its production to U.S. soil, and agreeing to administer treatment to the mentally disabled as defined by the NIH. John had given it a fifty-fifty chance that the government would agree to these terms, and he thought it wisest to take this course, as the cost would be minimal and the court proceedings would be short.

Another fixation was troubling Daniel. He'd been sleepless thinking about how the 5hmC Titan would behave in zero gravity and what would happen if it were self-replicated in synthetic XNA. He suspected that mutation would grow longer stint and more robust connection in vacuum, but how would it help? This question kept on surfacing in his head and taking over his real dilemma: the government.

Researchers in outer space had successfully developed twelve synthetic alternatives to human genetic molecules that were capable of storing and transmitting information. Dubbed XNA, this new genetic mix was capable of undergoing evolution. It was a huge breakthrough that meant RNA and DNA were no longer the only candidates capable of evolving and building life-forms. The creation of XNA suggested that it was likely, from an evolutionary standpoint, that neither RNA nor its probable successor, DNA, was the original replicator in the primordial "soup" of life. This prompted the theory that RNA and DNA evolved from earlier, simpler replicators. The X in XNA stood for *xeno-*, which was derived from the ancient Greek prefix meaning "alien" or "foreign."

At Stanford there was an entire field of study called exobiology, a discipline adopted in 2038. Daniel had taken one class in the subject but had deemed it too theoretical and close to science fiction. Exobiologists investigated the potential for life outside Earth and the impact of extraterrestrial environments on organisms. But Daniel's mind was on the move again. Maybe now it was time to revisit XNA. What if he could harvest the so-called intelligence gene, HMGA2, and overlay it on his memristor? Could that create a super boost in the human brain, far beyond the needs of the disabled?

HMGA2 had been discovered years ago at UCLA by Dr. Paul Thompson in a project called ENIGMA (Enhancing Neuro Imaging Genetics through Meta-Analysis). Dr. Thompson's research had begun much as Daniel's had: he'd been looking for gene markers for hereditary disorders like schizophrenia, bipolar disorder, depression, Alzheimer's disease, and dementia. In the end, his hard work paid off: he discovered HMGA2, the common DNA variant (a change in a single DNA base). In his ENIGMA project he employed measurements of the brains and memory centers from thousands of MRI images of over 20,000 healthy people, all while simultaneously screening their DNA.

Anaya had called to check on Daniel. Aside from his attorneys, she knew the most about his research. Now he felt he could tell her about the zero-gravity experiment that he wanted to conduct. Anaya had a close friend named William who worked as a contractor for the military. His company, WMH Corporation, made conceptual vehicles for the U.S. Defense Department, in addition to working on a few secret projects. Anaya asked if she could tell William about Daniel's work. Knowing that William was trustworthy and might have a different take on his trouble with the patent matter, Daniel agreed.

A short while later William called, and the two talked for over an hour. Daniel entrusted him with all his plans and apprehensions. William said he knew a low-level employee of Livermore Lab. She worked in the same department as Dr. Wu, but she was at the aerospace missile desk. What Daniel found most helpful about the conversation was learning that the government, posturing aside, was in a very weak position indeed. William told him about private conversations he'd had with a MHD staffer once, and he had discovered the government's vulnerability, especially prior to bringing an inventor on board, and especially while in negotiations with that inventor.

"The government's Achilles' heel is the word *public*," William told Daniel. "All you have to do is utter that word, and they will buckle and moderate their position. It makes sense that any leaks to the public would be detrimental to their modus operandi; the idea of the government interfering with private citizens' research on cures for the ill, demanding ownership and control over their patents, trampling on their hard labor, inhibiting their creativity, and offering hush money would certainly cause concern. Such news could be blown out of proportion if details were made public; it could instigate outrage and, with a little media attention, it could be portrayed as a blow to the free-enterprise system. It could even weaken the credibility of the entire military.

A decision needed to be made soon. By the time John Massetti called, Daniel had become much more confident and relaxed. He suggested that John not respond to the patent office on time. "Let them sweat a little," Daniel said.

"Do you know anything I should know?" John replied.

"Well, John, I've been thinking. If I were ever to feel hopeless and taken advantage of, as I sort of do now, I would broadcast what has happened on my RadGio for the entire world to hear. If I did that to the USPTO, it would be too late for them to stop me. John, they need to know that I am fearless, not just a nerd with great ideas."

Daniel seemed to have played his best card yet. John paused, sighed deeply, and said, "Have you been talking with anyone? Where did that come from?" Then, lacking a response from Daniel, he continued, "If that is the course of action you want to take, you do not need my advice anymore. I just want to let you know that you may be playing with fire, and it is my duty to caution you."

"I think you want the easy way out, John. I did not do all this research to be offered a job at Livermore Lab, that I can tell you."

"Well, what do you want under these circumstances?" John asked.

"I want a spot on the next SpaceX rocket to visit the International Space Station so that I can do more testing, that's what I want."

"Look, Daniel, you're not in any position to dictate space travels here. I will relay what you are saying anyway—you are my client—but I do not share your view. Please do me a favor and do not talk to anyone about this—I mean *anyone*."

"John, are you worried they will do something to hurt me? Well, it's too late. I have confided already to someone whose name I will never give up. I am disgusted about what the government is doing to private citizen and a patriot. I have documented all events thus far, and if they were to put me in a gulag or a reeducation camp, like in the old Soviet Union, it wouldn't work with me. This is ridiculous. They'll have to kill me . . . but the whole world will know why."

John shouted, "This is getting out of hand! I did not sign up for this, Daniel. I have to go now. I will call you later if I can help you—and that's a big 'if.'"

Daniel had played the hardball act to give John some motivation to negotiate, so John's belligerent reaction surprised him. Daniel had planned to make it a joke: he did not want to answer Dr. Wu just yet, and he really needed good advice on what to do. After testing John's reaction, he changed his tactic and became serious. There was something about John's tantrum that troubled him, perhaps a hint of apprehension at a deeper level. "What could it be?" he thought.

Since 2012, NASA had subcontracted with a private company called SpaceX to launch missions to the International Space Station (ISS). It was a win-win situation: the government saved money, while SpaceX improved their rockets and earned a perfect safety record. SpaceX not only ferried scientists to the space station, but also carried space tourists. The company made considerable money by charging reasonable rates that did not require passengers to be millionaires to take the eight-hour ride to see the heavens.

John wrote to Felix Curry, the government's attorney on the case, and told him that he would no longer represent Daniel because his client was "not heeding his counsel's advice and may refuse to cooperate in his own representation." Withdrawal from representation was generally frowned upon and, in some states, was not allowed if it were deemed to "injure" the client. In federal court, however, it was permissible to drop clients. Attorneys usually pulled out if they knew they were representing a guilty person, but before walking out they usually would try to lower the sentence. In this case, Daniel had not done anything criminal yet. Felix noticed another sentence in John's letter: he described his client as "unmanageable" and reported that he had "other reasons that I am not at liberty to disclose." The last part caught Felix's attention the most.

Before Felix could finish reading the letter, he received a call from John telling him that he planned to bow out and asking Felix to confirm in writing that John no longer represented Daniel Oakley. It was a simple request, since the two parties, Daniel and the government had exchanged hardly any legal documents, and there were no proceedings pending—practically speaking, there was no case yet. Felix said he would review John's request with the chief solicitor's office and promised to get back to him in the next day or two, but first he wanted John to elaborate on what he meant by "other reasons."

John replied, "I don't know what to tell you, but my ex-client thinks his case is some sort of a consumer complaint. I can't tell you what he'll do, and I can't say anymore, but I really want out."

Dropping clients at this early stage did not carry the usual ethical burden, but Felix was bothered by the conversation and the fact that he could not clear up what John meant by "other reasons," two words that attorneys used when they knew of a client's guilt or an impeding illegal action. The words had seemed particularly sinister when spoken on the phone. John had dropped another significant phrase, "consumer complaint." This could mean only one thing: Daniel intended to release the entire case to the media. It was obvious that John was trying to tell the government what his client was up to, and that's what worried everyone.

The news of John Massetti trying to quit reached Dr. Wu during a ceremony honoring disabled American veterans at the White House on the rainy evening of

83

November 23. It was a coincidence that some of the veterans the MHD was helping were themselves good candidates for Titan. Dr. Wu wasted no time. He went into a hallway, where he found the military top brass, Secretary of Defense Philip H. Sheridan, and George Aliki, a brigadier major general whom he knew very well.

Dr. Wu and George Aliki had crossed paths in Rome during a hasty NATO summit on May 18, 2022, after China announced that it had more satellites orbiting Earth than all the NATO countries combined. China had timed its announcement to coincide with the inauguration of a grand wing attached to the ISS. The lavish wing, which had its own private docking facility allowing only Chinese-made rockets and spacecraft to dock, was nicknamed Chinatown by the West. It had been a struggle for the UN to keep China in the fold, and a last-minute deal worked out by the UN Security Council had prevented China from building its own entire space station.

Dr. Wu was visiting a pharmaceutical company at the Rome summit when he was rushed to review some classified materials received by a Taiwanese secret agent about a recent claim from China that scientists could alter human DNA signatures to make a new identity on a person making him impossible to track. The Chinese called it the X treatment. Dr. Wu and George had a closed-door discussion at the Pantheon, away from the heads of state. The Pantheon was a fitting symbol of Western civilization's continuity. It had been chosen as a meeting site partly for the sake of psychological public relations — to reach the Chinese and remind them of Western civilization's magnificent history, in a not-so-subtle comeback to China's recent national euphoria.

Through its propaganda, the Chinese government had been making an effort to elevate its population's morale. In a sinister effort to keep the people in line with the ruling party, officials had been broadcasting China's historical achievements, beginning with the earliest Xia dynasty through the building of the Great Wall. This celebration, along with the announcement of the private outer-space lab, made a great impression on the Chinese psyche by emphasizing the nation's well-deserved superiority. Western diplomats privately compared the Chinese media blitz to Goebbels's actions during World War II, when he practiced mass deception against Germans.

Dr. Wu and George Aliki had kept in touch. Recently George had asked Dr. Wu if he had any openings in his lab for his daughter Yana to do an internship in her field, microbiology. Today, at the White House ceremony, Dr. Wu whispered in George's ear that he needed to talk to him urgently. The rain prevented them from walking outside, but in the hallway Dr. Wu was able to brief George about Daniel Oakley's Titan project. Both men concluded that Daniel's attorney had clearly hinted that he was excusing himself for one reason only: Daniel was going to make his story public, very likely on RadGio, and the consequences would be devastating.

George wasted no time. He briefed the secretary of defense on the brewing problem with Daniel Oakley, as he was known to be approachable. He built up the danger without providing all the facts, which hopefully would alarm the secretary enough to get the president involved.

It was essential that Director of Defense Sheridan hear the story from Dr. Wu, so George arranged for a meeting the following day at the Pentagon. Dr. Wu, however, asked that the matter be considered an urgent national security issue that needed immediate attention. George waved for Dr. Wu to come forward, and after the formal greetings, Dr. Wu said, "Secretary Sheridan, I cannot stress enough how damaging it may be if the public becomes aware of this matter; George may have told you that the inventor seems to be a good kid—an arrogant one, maybe, at the least—but we can't allow him to be out in the open, sir. We just can't."

Secretary Sheridan replied, "Well, we can't put people in jail without due process; we are not in China or the USSR, I am, however, prepared to ask the president. Hang in there."

The secretary left the hall, approached the security desk on the opposite side of the ballroom, and asked if he could see the president for about five minutes. "Please relay that it's an urgent matter," he told the officer in charge. In the White House, protocol required notifying the chief of staff of such matters. The chief of staff then decided whether to make an appointment on behalf of the president, sometimes without the president's knowledge. It did not take very long for Secretary Sheridan to receive a secure message on his Phonepad summoning him to the Oval Office.

Chapter 5

A National Hero

The secretary entered the president's office and got right to the point. "Mr. President, I hate to disturb you, but we have a renegade inventor named Daniel Oakley who has apparently devised some sort of method, and the head of HMD is extremely worried that it will become public."

The president said with his usual sarcasm, "What do you want me to do, kill the guy?" A smirk formed on his round face.

"Absolutely not, and I realize you don't mean it, sir."

The president fired back, "Seriously, what do you want me to do as president? We have agencies on top of other agencies, plus an MHD office, where these matters are resolved, am I right?"

"You are absolutely correct, sir. As a matter of fact, the head of the MHD, who alerted us all to this matter, is here. He's right down the hall in the ballroom, sir."

"Well, then, bring him over now. Isn't that what you want to do? I have no problem talking to that person. I can't remember his name, honestly." The president waved to his chief of staff, Mrs. Lancaster.

"Will do, sir," said Mrs. Lancaster. "I will fetch him for you, but can anyone tell me a name?"

"Dr. Wu," Secretary Sheridan replied.

Dr. Wu appeared pale and shaken. It was the first time he'd met the president one-on-one. He had met with him once, and they had shaken hands during the inauguration of the massive new wing of the nuclear microbiology building at Livermore a year earlier, but they had never actually spoken.

The president began by saying, "Look, Dr. Wu, I am not going to get into the details of this invention, because frankly I won't understand it. Give me the thirty-second version without getting too technical."

"Well, Mr. President, the invention has to do with a new type of memory chip that is coated with healthy DNA material that gains formidable power, function, and memory. The chip gets attached to the outside of the brain and is connected to the exact spot that needs help. Although it was conceived to help folks with brain damage and other disabilities, we strongly believe that it can affect normal folks as well."

"You mean dumb folks like us," the president joked.

Dr. Wu nodded. "Sir, if we are to believe the data generated from Mr. Oakley's experiments, as well as the claims he's made in his patent application, we conclude that his invention would have a profound effect on the population in general. If the chip were allowed to become public knowledge and to reach the market, sir, the answer is yes, it would affect normal people. It could also lead to a contest to obtain Mr. Oakley's device under the guise of improving memory, motor function, or any other aspect of the brain. Mr. President, if you tap the proper areas of the brain, you can essentially have human robots with encyclopedic knowledge walking the streets. That is what—"

The president interrupted. "You mean to tell me there is potential for superhumans, like in the movies?"

Dr. Wu replied, "That is a big possibility, sir."

President Lieberman got up and said, "I want to meet this guy. As a country we are proud to produce folks like that, aren't we? Aren't you glad he's in America?"

"We are, sir, but he's told his attorney that he's going public with his idea, against the good advice he's been given."

Quickly and instinctively, the president said, "I will gladly host this Oakley here at the White House, insist that he cooperate with you folks in the interest of the country, and slap him with a medal or two. It can be public. He's got to love that, right? We don't have to tell anyone any of these crazy details. We can give him the — what do you call it? — the National Medal of Science. From the sound of it, heck, the guy deserves it."

There was a hush in the Oval Office. It seemed as if the president had lived up to his reputation of being witty, sincerely admiring personal achievement, and rewarding it as best he could. To him, making a hero of an inventor meant that the United States could claim intellectual supremacy. The president genuinely wanted to reward success; it was a direct tribute to the Founding Fathers who created a glorious constitutional democracy, thus allowing the American genius to flourish. The president had meant what he'd said in his speech to the veterans down the hall: he would "not leave a stone unturned or shy away from budget squabbles to prevent you from having the best medicine and treatments the world can provide, a token contribution for your service to this great nation." He was aware that technological advancements, in terms of new inventions and products on the market, had begun to drop ten years earlier. What had been a solid lead in terms of patent filing, with 74 percent of worldwide applications from the United States five years earlier, had diminished to 59 percent. Still, it was an impressive number for a country of 375 million people compared to the entire world population of 8.5 billion.

The president got up and asked, "What do you say, Secretary Sheridan? I'll put some sense into this guy. What's his background, anything out of the ordinary? He's got to like his country and not want it to come to any harm. Like I said, we'll give him an award from Congress too, with some cash, exposure, and fame, in exchange for working with us and keeping his mouth shut—a win-win, don't you gentlemen think?"

The secretary of defense replied, "I agree, Mr. President. His background is clean-cut—good old American, from what I have been told. I do suggest, however—and Dr. Wu, you can correct me if I'm wrong—that the call be made to his attorney instead of to Oakley himself."

The president asked Mrs. Lancaster to call Daniel's attorney and to see if Daniel Oakley could come on the line as well.

John Massetti could not believe his ears when he heard from the chief of staff. Mrs. Lancaster told him that the president wanted to speak with Daniel and, if that were not possible, to have John relay the message that the White House was going to present his client with the National Medal of Science, and Daniel needed to contact Secretary of Defense Sheridan. Mrs. Lancaster passed on the secretary's direct contact information and said she hoped they would hear from Mr. Oakley that day. John asked if he could be on the invitation list for the ceremony. She agreed, provided that no government officials objected. Mrs. Lancaster hastily set up the ceremony for January 11, 2027, at 2:30 p.m. in the Vermeil Room on the first floor of the White House.

In the meantime, Daniel had begun to feel down on himself. He wondered if he was taking the aggressive act too far. He never meant to go public, and the only reason he had mentioned the threat to his attorney was to create a legitimate quid pro quo to even the balance in the negotiation that he thought was inevitable. His bluff seemed to have backfired, especially when John had shown no tolerance for playing that game. His personal experience with the government had exhausted his negotiation skills and limited his humor bandwidth. He was not prepared to put the word *public* on the table, now that he knew it would be like calling "Fire!" in a crowded theater, with all its serious consequences. But when John got hold of Daniel, it seemed like their confrontation had never happened.

John began with a heartfelt greeting. "Daniel, how have you been?"

"Good. What's up?"

"Well, have you told anyone about Titan?"

"Why do you ask?"

"Just tell me," said John. "You might like what I have to say."

"Let me say that I plead the Fifth on that. You know, if something were to happen to me, the whole world would know why, John. I mean it. I don't want to repeat myself. I am disgusted by how they are strong-arming a guy like me. I just don't like to be taken for a fool. Yes, I have made a sort of encrypted will, destined to be found by certain people to make sure that after I'm gone they will be very sorry."

It seemed that Daniel had not given up on leveraging his position to the very end, a game who's ending he did not see and whose rules of engagement he did not know. He would take it one day at a time.

"Whoa, whoa. Hear me out, please," said John. "How would you like to meet the president?"

"Which one? Our president?"

"Yes, Daniel, the U.S. president. You have been invited to receive the National Medal of Science award. The ceremony will be public, but there will be no details given to anyone, except to say that your excellent research and findings are meant to help the disabled. At this point I would be glad if no one has heard about your decision to go public. Do you see where I'm coming from?"

"The answer is . . . well . . . I don't know what people have heard, but absolutely, yes, I would love to meet the president. Thank God I voted for him."

John filled Daniel in on all the ceremony details and assured him, "I will be there by your side. I'll even go pro bono."

Daniel asked, "Is anyone talking about the job offer from Livermore? How did this reward come about? What's the mechanism for selecting scientists? And how on Earth did anyone on a selection committee find out about what I've done based on a two-week-old Stanford publication and a patent application that's less than three months old?"

John replied, "No one is talking about a job contract yet, but I suspect they will soon. As for their knowledge of your invention, there are lots of ways to know. The Stanford publication is read by people high up the chain of command. Besides, we're talking about folks who make it their job to snoop around. Anyway, who cares? This is a great opportunity, an honor, and a privilege, and I beg you not to ask me too many questions. I am told you can bring your parents if you want."

Daniel's mood swung, and within minutes he was back to his old jolly self. His parents were very happy to hear the good news. Robert could not control his jubilation; he broadcasted it on RadGio, and soon there was a flood of calls to everyone in the family. Robert felt vindicated that his country had not failed his son; Daniel's creative genius had earned one of the highest medals in his field the good old-fashioned way. Ama could not help but spread the news about the award while cooking her various dishes on TV. She joked to her audiences that her recipes had her son's stamp of approval. "He's a scientist who plays with DNA, and he knows best," she said. "He's going to the White House to get a medal."

It was essential that John Massetti keep in touch with Felix Curry, the government counsel. John assured Felix that to his knowledge, Daniel had not revealed his findings to anyone, but he had some sort of an encrypted will that John thought was a bluff—"The kid has seen too many movies. He thinks someone will take him out if he does not comply."

"Well, you can't blame him, John. He's paranoid now. It is your job to keep representing him; he'll need you " Felix called Dr. Wu, and they agreed that it was time to make another attempt through John to have Daniel sign the employment contract. As a last resort, they wanted the president to help put some sort of a "leash" on Daniel, as they termed it. Felix and Dr. Wu also agreed that the medal business was premature and hasty. They wondered if there was a credible way to make the medal conditional on Daniel's agreement to work for them—to get Daniel's signature on the contract first. They figured they would test the waters with John. It was unclear to them how, after a fifteen-minute ceremony, the president could convince Daniel to cooperate unless they sat in a closed-door session with the secretary of defense to help make the case. Daniel had proved to be a shrewd player thus far. Eventually they decided they would have no choice but to rely on Daniel's good nature—that after his experiences at the White House, he would find it hard not to work with the government.

The weather was surprisingly mild in Washington when everyone gathered in the Vermeil Room. The president stood at the center of the hall and delivered a short and eloquent speech. He praised "the free-enterprise system and the individual liberties that Americans enjoy, that were etched in the rocks of liberty by our Founding Fathers, who enabled this country to produce talent and inventions that have been the cornerstones of modern humanity. The incredible human capital that this country possesses has proved time and again that quality will always fare better than quantity, especially when it gives birth to folks like Dr. Daniel Oakley. We celebrate his contribution today, and with great honor I bestow the National Medal of Science on the youngest recipient in our history."

The president's speech brought tears to Daniel's parents' eyes. It was carried live on most major networks. The invitation list included an extensive selection of the press, executives from drug companies, and nongovernmental organization (NGO) heads.

At the ceremony Daniel spotted a beautiful young woman wearing a dark purple business suit. She was speaking in foreign language to people he thought were from India. On the left side of her collar was a pin that read CC; CHILDREN'S CHAMPION. He could not help but notice her large, dark eyes and her silky, long hair; at first glance she reminded him of Mirvet.

She approached him with a businesslike manner and congratulated him on his achievement—"even though I frankly don't know what it is, exactly."

Daniel replied, "Well, I wish I could explain it—I mean, I can't, myself. Can you tell me about CC—your button?"

"We help children worldwide. Children's Champion is an NGO based in Rome. I challenge you to explain what you are doing. You might be surprised that I am capable of understanding your world. I have a master in microbiology."

"I don't mean it that way," Daniel said quickly. "It is just that sometimes it's hard to give a forty-second version of a big project."

"Well, I can spare more time than that if you can."

She had a gorgeous smile, and Daniel took notice. He blushed and nervously said, "Yes, we can talk about that over a drink someday."

"I would love that. I am here for a few more days. I'm Francesca, by the way."

"What language were you speaking?"

"Urdu."

"Are you from India?"

"No, I am Italian, but I lived in India. My father was the Italian ambassador in Mumbai."

"Fascinating. I will call you, I promise, and we'll only speak English."

They did a quick virtual handshake on their Phonepads via RadGio to exchange their public domains and bios, followed by an actual handshake.

Daniel spotted Dr. Wu, approached him with a confident handshake, and said with a teasing tone, "Dr. Wu, I didn't know you were invited here."

"It's good to actually meet you in person, Dr. Oakley. You know, with these 3-D cameras on Phonepads, I can't pretend that you look any different—taller, maybe, but not different. Well, I think Secretary Sheridan wants to talk with you. I believe he secured a private meeting for you and the president. Now, on *that* one I am not invited, if it makes you feel better."

Daniel replied, "Look, nothing against you, but I don't kneel to anyone against my will, including my beloved country."

"I think you may be making a big deal out of nothing, Mr. Oakley. You'll be surprised how everyone, including myself, wants the best for you. You know, there is a little cash award for you from Congress. Did they ask for your PayGeo?"

"As a matter of fact, they did."

Secretary Sheridan walked over with John Massetti and touched Daniel's elbow. He said, "The famous Dr. Oakley, what an honor. Do your smarts come from your mom's cooking, or what?"

"No, sir. If my mom's food could make you smarter, our cat Zoe could have become president."

A robust laugh poured out of the four men gathered in the center of the room, and Daniel continued. "I mean no insult, of course. I voted for our president."

It seemed the noise of their laughter had been a call for strangers to begin a photo-taking session with Daniel and people he had never seen. A few minutes later, the secretary of defense said, "Well, well, we have a comedian on top of it all, Dr. Wu. You don't find a well-rounded scientist with a sense of humor in this day and age—maybe in past centuries, but not anymore. It is refreshing to meet you, Mr. Oakley."

"Thank you, sir. I'll apologize for my joke if you think it necessary."

"Heck, not at all! I just might steal it and tell the president myself. Would you mind?"

"I wouldn't mind, but I would want a signed disclaimer that if he were to get upset and excuse your services, you wouldn't blame me for anything."

Secretary Sheridan laughed. "You are a witty young man. I think the president is going to like you. Well, speaking of signing disclaimers, I think the president might be talking about something similar. You do know that we have a few minutes with him in the Oval Office?"

"Yes, I was told that."

They walked past the security desk and proceeded to some wide-open double doors. Only Daniel and the secretary of defense were scheduled for the meeting. John had tried to be included but had been refused because the meeting was a "purely private audience with no legal merit"as the secretary told him. They entered the Oval Office. The president walked up, shook hands with Daniel and Secretary Sheridan, and invited both to sit on the chairs facing his desk.

"Welcome home, Dr. Oakley," the president began. "The White House belongs to the nation and is for everyone, you know?" This was a line that the president repeated to private visitors, veterans, and nonprofit organizations alike. It seemed like a sensible motto, as it reminded his visitors that he was working for the people.

Daniel replied, "Thank you, Mr. President. I assume that just you should stay in the White house sir, you earned your votes, besides I can't afford it here sir, but I am honored that you want to speak with me"

"You are funny guy. No one mentioned that to me. Secretary Sheridan?"

"Sir, wait till you hear his joke from just a few minutes ago," the secretary began.

Daniel interrupted politely. "Mr. President, it's not my joke anymore; Secretary Sheridan asked for it, and I have forfeited it."

The president said, "I do want to hear your joke, but first I want to make one thing clear to you, Dr. Oakley—and I want Secretary Sheridan to follow up. I know that you may be thinking that we, the government, are pushing you into a corner, Dr. Oakley. I don't want you ever to feel that way. I have you sitting here to tell you that experienced folks in this administration have deemed your invention a national security issue. Now, you may disagree with that, and that is your prerogative, but it so happens that the risk outweighs the benefit in letting—what do you call it?—your chip . . ."

"Titan," Daniel offered.

"Right. Cool name. Letting the Titan onto the streets, so to speak, is dangerous for us as a country and for our loved ones, and from that perspective, I want you to cooperate with Philip here and put this matter to bed. Agreed?"

Sweat had sprung on Daniel's forehead. He had zoomed in on the president's demeanor while listening, unconvinced of his polite assertion. "Mr. President, I repeat that I am honored, and I agree now that the government has the right to put a lock on Titan. The problem, as I see it, is that they are putting a lock on me. And even though I agree with their right to demand such a lock, I don't necessarily agree that I don't have the right to object to it, sir."

Secretary Sheridan interrupted. "Daniel, no one is talking about locks. Where did you come up with that? We have an employment letter that spells out certain parameters that are necessary for the security of this country, while guaranteeing you the opportunity to continue working and—who knows?—come up with another new invention. Don't think of locks, please."

Daniel continued. "If I may say, Mr. President, all I ask is that we all abide with the speech that you just made down the hall."

"What are you referring to, Dr. Oakley?" asked President Lieberman.

"The part that talked about individual liberties etched on rocks by our Founding Fathers."

The president, hiding his embarrassment, said, "Oh, God, my speechwriters have done it again. With a forced grin, he continued. "Look, Doc, hopefully someday you'll sit in my chair, or in some other ones that give you responsibility beyond yourself and your family. Imagine that the entire country's security is at stake, and from that angle, I ask that you cooperate. I can't demand that you cooperate — you are not a public employee, and even if you were, nowadays it's hard to make anyone do anything — right, Philip?"

"Yes, Mr. President, I agree. We just need to put this matter to bed, guarantee that our star sitting with us here can feel good about working with us, about protecting his rights, and so on. And it's not hard — we are preparing a toned-down employment contract, without all the legalese mumbo jumbo, for Dr. Oakley to sign. We were going to give it to him before the medal ceremony, but we knew how sensitive this matter was and did not want him to feel that we're buying his great service to this country. See, Daniel, we are not these mean, big, bad wolves. We're not. We want what's best for everyone, including you. By the time you head back to California, your attorney will have this new document on his desk, and we ask that you kindly sign it and get this thing behind us. Mr. President, if I may presume that you are our star witness, and again Daniel, I want you to promise that you'll comply"

Daniel had no choice but to agree. He replied, "All right. Based on what I have heard, I will comply."

The president got up and said, "I need to hear the joke before you go, Daniel."

"No, sir, it is not mine. Secretary Sheridan, go ahead."

The president did not find the joke too amusing, but he said, "That's the best joke I've heard all day."

Daniel had always wanted to go to the Smithsonian Institution, and he asked Francesca to meet him there. There were fine restaurants in that area, and if they got along, they could spend quality time there. Francesca met him at the main entrance of this grand structure, which looked like the front of the White House. Funded by the government, the Smithsonian had a budget of two billion G ($2.5 billion). The organization began in the 1820s as a donation from an English gentleman scientist who never visited America, with the purpose of creating an "Establishment for the increase & diffusion of Knowledge among men." After the scientist's last supervising heir had died, the U.S. government took full control after lengthy debates about whether gifts of this sort could be accepted. Finally, on July 1, 1836, Congress accepted the legacy "bequeathed to the nation" and pledged the faith of the United States to the "Charitable trust of the Smithsonian."

They chose to see the National Museum of Natural History, home to a magnificent collection from all corners of the earth, especially Kenneth E. Behring's exhibit featuring lifelike poses of mammals in their natural habitats. It had been over twenty years since Daniel had gone to the museum with his mother while visiting her relatives in Virginia, and it was the first time for Francesca. It did not take long for the couple to feel a certain warmth. The chemistry seemed right for lame scientific jokes; one comment from Daniel, who said he wished that he had a mammal to work with at Stanford, particularly caught his date's attention.

Francesca asked several questions about Daniel's research. He was careful to give her a simplified overview, not due to her lack of capacity to understand — he found her very intelligent — but for the sake of keeping the peace with the government and minimizing the supposed danger of anyone knowing about Titan. She seemed impressed, so he let it be.

Francesca's attraction toward Daniel was obviously reciprocated. He asked her detailed questions about the work of Children's Champion. Francesca's job was to raise funds, mostly from pharmaceutical firms and the government, and to complete the many tedious applications for the UN to comply with funding mandates. When Daniel asked her to name the best and kindest drug company, which truly cared about the children's best interest in addition to making a profit, he was surprised that, without any hesitation, she named Respi, a Rome-based company that stood out from the rest. Daniel became curious about what Respi did differently, and he wanted to know if its shareholders were especially good people. He was surprised yet again to find out that the company remained private and in the hands of actual owners whom Francesca knew personally; she had grown up and attended college with the owner's son, Marco, and she had done an internship at Respi before accepting the job at CC.

The company had been founded in 1999 by a young scientist named Ricardo Montalcini. He had won a Nobel Prize for working on homologous recombination, a process that cells use to repair their own DNA, and that scientists exploit to turn genes off and on in order to make advanced genetic drugs. The Italian government had provided a substantial loan back then, and Montalcini's research had panned out. Ultimately he had made some drugs of his own, as well as licensing other companies to make different medicines that were researched at Respi. Francesca indicated that the Montalcini family, although wealthy, remained humble and sought to help children worldwide. Respi was currently CC's biggest contributor.

Daniel said, "I'd love to meet with Respi's principals one day. Do you think you could help me with that?"

"Absolutely," Francesca replied. "I can arrange a meeting — you mean in person, right?"

"Yes, I am tired of talking to screens. In person would be best."

"Do you think you'd want to live in Italy?"

"I have never been there in my adult life. I went to the top tourist spots with my parents when I was in my teens — Venice, Pisa, Florence, Rome, the Vatican. . . . I liked it then, but I can't honestly tell you if I'd like living there."

There was an awkward silence. Then Francesca said, "If you liked someone there, then you'd want to stay, no?"

"I suppose you're right. . . ."

As they left the Smithsonian garden, a cold chill took them by surprise. It seemed both had the same idea, and they walked against the wind in an uncomfortable cuddle.

They reached the cafés at the opposite end of the plaza and sat down to have a short meal and a warm drink. They had spent most of the day together and had gotten unusually close for a first date. Using the excuse of keeping warm, they clutched their hands together. Daniel was not shy this time around; he picked up Francesca's hand, rubbed it on his face, and kissed it.

She pulled her hand back quickly and said, "You're making my hands too warm."

Daniel replied, "You're too hot for *me*. I would love to see you again."

Francesca recoiled and said that although she was not seeing anyone, there was no reason to rush a relationship — she would be leaving tomorrow. Then she admitted, "I'd like to give you a reason to come to Rome, though. What do you say?"

"I think I should learn Italian, pronto."

A beautiful smile lit up Francesca's face, and without hesitation, Daniel gave her a passionate kiss on the lips and said "fate will bring us together again, and if not, I will ask fate to do it"

Back at his parents' house, Daniel had a lot of material to cover. John had presented him with a new government employment contract, placing him at the head of a new department at Livermore Lab. The contract contained improved language to protect Daniel's rights. It allowed him to question the head of the HMD office on decisions related to research, development, and production, while making the secretary of defense a quasi arbitrator. However, the government kept the same restrictions on Daniel's ability to receive commercial or royalty rewards, and there was no specific time frame for his release from these restrictions. Also on Daniel's mind was his romantic vision of working with Respi, having the freedom to conduct research unhindered, and spending time with Francesca.

Daniel and Francesca kept in touch constantly on RadGio, and soon he got careless. He would say things like, "I am not clear on what the government wants to do with my research." "I am being bullied by bureaucracy." "Sometimes I wish I could pack up and go somewhere where I can do work in peace. At one point he sarcastically quipped, "Give me liberty or give me death!"

Daniel agreed to Francesca's request that he meet Marco, the CEO of Respi. During these decisive three weeks, while constantly talking to Daniel about anything and everything, Francesca got to know him very well. They had charming and loving conversations; for instance, she would say, *"Sono dipendente dei tuoi baci"* ("I am addicted to your kisses"). Daniel began to teach himself Italian and was able to respond with competing phrases such as *"Tu sei l'unico per me"* ("You're the only one for me").

Marco was extremely cordial when he and Daniel had their first meeting on the Phonepad, with Francesca present to make the introduction. Daniel felt at ease; having Francesca on the call helped make it informal. Marco, who spoke perfect English with a British accent, congratulated Daniel on the medal. He had received his master's degree in microbiology at Cambridge, England.

After the initial pleasantries, Marco quickly got to the point. He invited Daniel to come to Rome to see if Daniel could "find a fit with our culture here at the company and in Italy in general."

Daniel replied, "I would no doubt love Italian culture, and from what Francesca has told me about Respi, I think I would like it as well." Daniel did not think twice about being honest; it seemed appropriate given his and Marco's backgrounds.

Francesca had fallen in love, and with traditional Italian passion, she needed Daniel to be by her side. She insisted that Daniel come to Italy for a face-to-face meeting with Marco. Daniel was under pressure from John to sign off on the offer from the U.S. government; it needed to happen fast. Daniel told John that he needed just a few more days to review it. John reminded him of his promise to the president and the fact that his credibility was on the line—after all, according to John, the changes to the contract had been "more than accommodating."

But this was still not enough for Daniel. His celebrity status had drawn many offers to the table. A few came from Europe, one was from India, and another was from Xi'an Pharmaceuticals in China. In the body of the letter, signed "The Chief of Staff," Xi'an had promised "an updated laboratory for continuing your research, without hindrance from the company." The salary was set at one million G, not including an exclusive flat in the newly built Shenzhen Tek-city. While Daniel's confidence had grown, his attorney felt Daniel was stonewalling him and dragging his feet for no good reason.

On the evening of February 12, Daniel finished dinner with his parents, turned around to Robert, and said, "I have decided to take a long trip, Dad. I am being pushed into a corner to work at Livermore, and frankly, I don't enjoy it. I don't trust the people there, so I am going to hop around the world and go on some interviews. There may be times when you don't hear from me, but please don't be alarmed."

Robert was elated. He thought that Daniel had earned this luxury. He had money in the bank, thanks to the handsome reward from Congress. As Robert saw it, Daniel's only worry was to stay out of trouble and not get entangled with foreign women. "By the way, son," Robert asked, "which way are you flying, east or west?"

"I'm not sure, Dad."

Ama had a different take. A sad look came over her, and with a soft voice she said, "Livermore is close, the weather is nice, and it's your home here. Besides, aren't you supposed to answer these people?"

"I am, Mom, but I am not going to be pressured, and as much as I appreciate the medal, I am beginning to feel that the award was hush money. I don't feel good about this. I'm not the kind of guy to work on a military base, pandering to bureaucrats. You guys know me."

"Well, how long will you be gone?"

Daniel avoided the question. "Look, Mom, the world is so small. Heck, in six hours we were in Egypt!"

"Are you going to Egypt?"

"No, I'm not. I had no job offers from there."

"Well, can't you tell us how long you're going to be gone? Robert, give us *some* idea."

Robert spoke up. "He's grown up, Ama. I'm not worried. Let him live his life. We're proud of you, son, but can you give your mom an idea of how long this trip will take? If you leave without me asking you, she'll be upset with me . . . so please, for my sake, tell us something."

Robert replied, "I am going to pursue every job offer that tickles my fancy — meet the people, see the labs, check out the weather, you know."

"And the ladies?" asked Robert.

"Yes, Dad, I will look over everything, including the ladies, the culture, and the living conditions. I won't feel good if I'm living the high life but walking out onto a street where beggars are around. I will make a good choice. Besides, I might end up down here in South San Francisco. David's a great brother-in-law — he said he could find me a spot in an instant. I might leave tomorrow, depending on what I have to do. I have open standby 15,000 miles tickets. There are flights from San Francisco and San Jose to practically anywhere I want. I might head east, towards Europe and can only promise to stay out of trouble… if trouble leaves me alone"

Chapter 6

Courting Daniel

Daniel landed in Rome at Fiumicino Airport on the evening of February 14. He had told Francesca to meet him. He was traveling light. He had uploaded his entire Phonepad to xcloud, a maximum-security database, as the thought of losing it was too disturbing. The Phonepad contained not just his contacts, but also his private PayGeo accounts—which he had intentionally set up with private companies worldwide—and his entire collection of research and patent documents for Titan.

PayGeo accounts had been around for over twenty years. They enabled money transfer between members, who could also access cash on ATM machines when they were popular. These days it was mostly used by young people to "park" their money, which earned minimal interest while digital G transfers and payments continued automatically.

Due to its great success, this system had mushroomed into a large payment platform. Cabs, restaurants, retail stores, and banks could scan 3-D codes generated by Phonepads, thus making it unnecessary for people to carry cash. Although the convenience won over millions of customers, there was a big controversy regarding the information that PayGeo provided to marketers and other agencies on the whereabouts of each customer and his or her buying habits. Lots of data was accumulated and sold. The World Bank had recently pushed through a new law prohibiting the sharing of all information on PayGeo accounts except in criminal investigations by governmental agencies backed by court orders. Privacy advocates had hailed the new law, and most people supported it. However, governments and big businesses had lobbied to keep access open.

As part of the World Growth Initiative mandated by the UN's thirty-two wealthiest countries, the World Bank allowed so-called money aggregators licenses to private companies to exchange money between members, as long as these companies did not invest more than 10 percent of available liquid assets. The idea was that hardworking people worldwide should not risk losing their money on banks' unscrupulous behavior, which amounted to over 1,800 bank failures alone in 2043, causing more than four hundred million people to lose their life's savings. These private PayGeo companies did not need a banking license in member countries, with the exception of the Dominican Republic—a nonmember state.

Governments argued that these types of accounts would encourage money laundering and tax evasion, by creating accounts owned by fictitious people having false identifications.

An agreement had been reached by the World Bank and PayGeo licensees only the previous month, and it would go into effect within ten days. It was still too new for Daniel to trust, so he asked Francesca to scan her account to get e-tickets for the train.

Rome was a lovers' paradise. Daniel and Francesca spent the weekend touring the landmarks of the city. After spending some intimate time together, Francesca could tell that Daniel had a lot on his mind—something terribly serious. It did not take very long for her to confront him. "Why are you making me pay with my Phonepad at all public places? Are you hiding from someone?" she asked.

"But I'm paying you back right afterward, sometimes with tip. Aren't you noticing the prompts on your PP?"

"I am, Daniel, but this is not an economic question. You use your own PP to pay in retail stores, but you have me use mine on any public transportation, at museums, and so on. Why?"

"You are smart, and that is why I am falling in love with you. I don't have a good answer, honestly. I left the U.S. with the intention of getting away, not letting anyone know where I was, not even my parents."

"But why?"

"Well, you know the pressure I am under. I am getting calls left and right. I feel like I'm being coerced into working at a place that I don't like. I just don't want to be found. Besides, I doubt anyone is looking for me."

"But what about yesterday's conversation with your attorney at two in the morning? I could hear everything, you know. You told him to go fly a kite. Is he a pilot as well?"

"You are too cute. That's a saying my dad taught me. It's slang for when you want people to go away and stop bothering you — you tell them to go fly a kite. Do you know what a kite is?"

"Oh, yes, I do, but why?"

"He wanted an immediate answer from me about joining Livermore Lab, and I said that I couldn't give him an answer. He insisted that the top dogs were after him, so I told him to have them fly a kite. That's all."

"Do you really think they don't know where you are?"

"Maybe. I'm not sure."

"You know, the government can look up the list of air travelers and know where everyone is in an instant, so, smarty, what would you do then?"

"I am not a fugitive, Francesca. I have not done anything wrong—not yet. I will use my PP to pay from now on; I think I am being childish."

"Yes, you are. Last time I checked, we live in a free society where you can choose your job, you know."

"Precisely. I am not going to play that game. You are right. Let me call my parents—my mom will be happy to hear where I am."

For the first time, Daniel's father sounded alarmed. "Where are you, son? What's going on?" he asked.

"Why do you ask, Dad? I'm in Rome."

"We had interesting visitors asking about you. They were from the military."

"What did they want?"

"Oh, besides wanting to know who you see, who your friends are, who you sleep with, who comes to the house, whether you have foreign friends, and whether you've received any paper mail or packages . . . nothing. They didn't want anything," said Robert with a sarcastic tone. "The funny thing is that they did not ask where you are, but when we told them that we don't know where you are, they thought we were lying. I think they know where you are, son. When they were at the door, they told us they had quick questions for you and us. They pretended they didn't know you were gone when we told them, but I could see the smirk on one of their faces. Look, please call your attorney, son. Let's not get tangled up with the law."

Daniel replied, "Last time I checked, we lived in a free country. I can go wherever I want. I spoke to John Massetti, my attorney, and I told him they can go to hell. I am looking for work, like any citizen is entitled to. I am not a government employee, Dad, so relax, please. Tell Mom not to worry."

John had alerted his counterpart in the government, Felix Curry, that Daniel, true to his nature, would not cooperate and that John was no longer representing him. The MHD office had had dealings with John years back and had made a secret agreement assigning John to a technical task force (TTF) reserve unit, whose main duty was to support government intelligence in a reserve capacity — it was called on when a civilian contractor was needed to do work that the military deemed nonessential, which usually meant that it could not do the work overtly.

This was not an uncommon arrangement. Beginning in the days of the Vietnam, Iraq, and other wars, people from all walks of life had been recruited to do contract work for the government. The idea was that it was cheaper to hire talent on an as-needed basis rather than inflating the government's payroll when no such tasks were required. What started as side-work jobs, such as building roads, supplying foodstuff, and transporting goods, morphed into jobs for special security personnel, computer hackers, intellectuals, and other specialized workers who were deployed to support clandestine operations. John had agreed to sign up for the TTF as part of his patent settlement ten years earlier. He had been called only once to report to his TTF reserve unit, based at Moffett Field, an old military base built in 1931 on the southern end of San Francisco Bay.

Later that morning, Felix told John that the government was going to invoke its right to enforce the TTF reserve unit rules such that John would have to continue his "representation" of Daniel, as it was necessary for John to find out what Daniel's next moves were under the pretext of giving him the "good advice" of the MHD. After all, Daniel had not, as of yet, asked John to stop representing him. On the surface it was a noble and defendable cause—an effort to "protect" Daniel from the big bad wolves that were trying to recruit him while also protecting the interests of the U.S. government. The MHD had no legal basis to stop Daniel, as he had managed to avoid signing any documents that tied him to the government. John, however, had no choice but to comply.

Francesca had set up a meeting for Daniel to see Marco at Respi's office complex in the town of Casalotti, a western suburb of Rome. Daniel sat in Marco's office with Marco, Francesca, and the head of the HR, Mrs. Antonella Fioretti. The tone was relaxed and congenial.

Marco remarked that it was the first time in his life that he had offered someone a job without reading his CV. A handsome man in his late forties, Marco had a striking intelligence and appeared very friendly. He joked that the word *CV* was antiquated. "Its literal translation from Latin is 'course of life,'" he said. "So, anyone who comes to work at Respi is choosing a course in his life that he hopes will benefit both the company and the individual."

"Fair enough," Daniel remarked. As the conversation had lacked any mention of compensation thus far, Daniel spoke about the freedom that he required while working in his lab—after all, he pointed out, he had a lot more interesting ideas that could come to fruition.

Marco pressed him on the point. "What is next, Daniel? Tell us, what would you be working on here at Respi if you were to accept our offer?"

Daniel tossed out a hint about his would-be projects. "I foresee XNA being big in the next century. If I can run experiments in zero gravity, I believe a new generation of XNA treatments would make a huge difference."

Zero-gravity experimentation had been carried on for decades at the ISS. The newly built Chinese wing had contributed respectable findings, especially in agricultural and bacterial research. Earth-based zero-gravity labs had been attempted with mediocre results; the new method invented by Indian scientist Varish Goyal had been the best so far. Dr. Goyal had created a capsule in which giant suction fans were placed on opposing walls. The fans took the air out of the chamber with tremendous vacuum force while employing magnetic electrostatic levitators embedded in the capsule walls, thus creating an environment of near-zero gravity. Such a lab was the closest on Earth to mimic the effects of the ISS—and Respi had one.

Daniel asked if he could take a tour of the lab. Mrs. Fioretti excused herself and passed her contact information to his RadGio Phonepad. Daniel could not help but be impressed with the entire setting and the calm and focused nature of everyone he met. He admitted to Marco that he needed to visit Shenzhen Tek-city to meet with another company. Marco smiled and said, "Let me guess. Xi'an Pharmaceuticals, no?"

"Correct," Daniel replied.

Marco put his hand on Daniel's shoulder and said, "Look, they are our competition, and we respect them very much, but I have to warn you that they deal with government agencies and weapons and all kinds of matters. From what I know about you, if I may say, you will not be happy there, regardless of the amount of money they pay. Look, we know people there who want to come work for us for half the money. But go and visit. You are a smart guy. See if you can spot these things. Go."

This part of the conversation was eye-opening for Daniel. He had no reason to doubt Marco. Francesca added to Marco's point by saying, "It's a different culture there. I have been there myself. It's very different, really, Daniel."

Meanwhile, Dr. Wu had become obsessed with getting the Daniel Oakley matter wrapped up. His most recent communication with George Aliki indicated that the secretary of defense was following the news closely. Secretary Sheridan had asked for a daily update on Dr. Oakley, or Titan Mater, as he had come to be known. Dr. Wu reported that they knew Daniel's whereabouts and believed that he might have accepted a job offer at the same pharmaceutical company that Dr. Wu had visited back in 2022, but there should be "no cause for alarm" at this stage.

Dr. Wu had indeed been at Respi, back when he and George had met during the NATO conference. Dr. Wu had kept in touch with Marco, the CEO. Respi was on the approved pharmaceutical company tenders' list, and they had done work on certain vaccines for the U.S. Army during the Azerbaijani crisis of 2018. Dr. Wu eventually conceded that he was, in fact, a bit worried and that his next move would be to contact Marco if John Massetti's effort to bring Daniel back failed. John was trying in vain to set up a conference call with Daniel, Dr. Wu, Felix, and himself, but Daniel was adamant about wanting no communication with anyone from the government under any circumstances. His rebellious mood had resurfaced, and John could report only on the scant information that Daniel would provide now and then. It was the same basic information that Dr. Wu had — except Dr. Wu's information was, without John Massetti's knowledge, far more detailed. His contribution amounted to gauging Daniel's mood, a relatively minor role in the big picture so far.

Marco was surprised to see that Dr. Wu had booked an urgent meeting and flew to Italy on a moment's notice; he found him waiting in the private conference room. Marco had figured there was a project of high importance that Dr. Wu needed to discuss, but on the calendar there were no listed attendees from Respi's various R & D and production departments.

Dr. Wu wasted no time in laying out the issue at hand. He purposely revealed a long list of projects that amounted to millions of euros. Then he emphasized the fact that Respi had been on his list of companies that he loved to do business with. Finally, he said there was a slight problem that he hoped Marco could help him with.

"Dr. Daniel Oakley," said Dr. Wu. After a deep breath, he continued. "We know that you may have hired him to work here. . . ."

"Is there a problem with him?" asked Marco.

"Oh, no, not a problem, but a potential one. He frankly misled President Lieberman after promising to work with us, with our own secretary of defense, Mr. Sheridan, as a witness. Well, he obviously changed his mind."

"With all due respect, Dr. Wu, can you force someone to work for you?" Marco was asking a sincere question.

"Well, no, we can't. We don't do forced-labor camps — we do not have a history like that, you know — but we expect our citizens to be truthful, and when they promise something, they ought to deliver. You know, I am here for a different reason, but this issue was thrown in my lap by higher-ups, and I have to deal with it. Marco, we are a civilized nation. We don't gag, kidnap, or force our private citizens to do anything when they don't break any laws. Dr. Oakley has not broken any laws thus far. He broke a promise, and that is not illegal per se. But I do expect you, as a partner and a vendor, to fulfill a certain fiduciary duty by keeping his project secret and informing us of the details of his daily work, by means of making his reports to his superior available to us. We will not be intrusive to you or your company, but once in a while we would like to listen in on a conversation or a meeting he's having. Did he mention the name of his work to you?"

"He mentioned Titan. Is that it?"

"Yes, that is it. You may not know how extremely confidential this thing is. Thank God he's in a fellow NATO country, and you guys understand the ramifications."

"If I may, Dr. Wu —"

"Sorry, Marco, let me just finish this. As part of my duty I must ask the Italian secret service to keep tabs on Daniel, and from what I understand, they have far more freedom than we do. Again, they will not be intrusive, but they can listen, track, and shadow anyone."

With a soft voice, Marco said, "Dr. Wu, Daniel has not committed to working here — not yet, at least. We offered him a deal that is beyond any scientist's dream, but he wanted a chance to look at Xi'an first."

Dr. Wu got up, put both hands on his head, and quickly apologized. "Sorry to have wasted your time, Marco." He paused for a minute and then walked out of the room without uttering another word.

Dr. Wu was furious. He thought of blaming John Massetti. It was a common practice within the government and the corporate world — faulting the immediate superior when a subordinate makes a mistake — but then Dr. Wu realized that the government had been trying to intercept Daniel's messages to no avail. Daniel had an advanced Phonepad with a built-in "kill pill" — an Intel chip that rendered the instrument useless if it fell into the wrong hands. In addition, he had chosen an encrypted chatting and working service that prevented even the MDI technicians from cracking his communication. No, Dr. Wu blamed the MDI for not knowing who had solicited Daniel's employment.

By the time Dr. Wu reached the St. Regis Rome, he had calmed down and realized that nothing legal could be done to prevent Daniel from going anywhere. Going to China for work was Daniel's mistake and no one else's. Carrying a medal from the U.S. president while working in China was a clear misrepresentation to everyone; it was nothing short of treason, Dr. Wu reckoned. Dr. Wu could see clearly Xi'an Pharmaceuticals, as well as the Chinese government, pulling a PR stunt—showing Daniel working for them of his own free will, laying out red carpets, and maybe even sending him to Chinatown (the newly built wing of the ISS).

"Daniel is just a kid. No doubt he will fall for that stuff. It's a darn shame," Dr. Wu thought. His next move was to put in an urgent call to the secretary of state.

Dr. Wu grew anxious and had trouble sleeping. Instead of taking a sleeping pill to overcome the change of time zone, he stayed up and called three people: George Aliki, the head of the CIA, and the White House chief of staff. He wanted to develop a coordinated plan to stop Daniel from going to China, but he did not want to suggest or authorize any move that he could be blamed for. He had no interest in becoming the fall guy.

The president was between meetings when the Mrs. Lancaster whispered that Secretary Sheridan needed to speak to him urgently. President Lieberman had very little patience for moles, whistle-blowers, and spies; he used one word, *backstabbers,* to describe them all.

Secretary Sheridan asked the president, "How do you suggest we stop him, sir?"

President Lieberman's response was quick: "You arrest him and bring him onto U.S. soil. If need be, an embassy of ours will do."

While the government had the right to detain prisoners or terrorists who were not U.S. citizens on a battlefield, or sometimes could bring to trial individuals outside war zones by making a case of "imminent danger," detaining a U.S. citizen was a different ball game.

The president called in his chief legal counsel, Andrew Kori, and in a calm and composed manner told him, "I have a job for you today. I have just authorized the detention of a U.S. citizen who is heading to China, presumably to give away some technology secrets of ours. I'm worried that this guy can cause some serious damage. You've got to find me some legal protection. Even if you don't, I am prepared to take the fall for the sake of the country, but I think you can be creative and find me some loophole."

"Mr. President," said Kori, "I've got the loophole here in my head. It's an actual law. Sir, the Supreme Court has already recognized the power of the government to detain a U.S. citizen and get the guy back in the country to talk to him. Under the 2014 anti-terrorism National Defense Act he needs to appear before an impartial civil judge once he's here. We can argue, Mr. President, that the information this guy has is akin to weapons or a weapons program that can be passed on to the enemy. Who is this guy, sir, if I may ask?"

"Dr. Daniel Oakley."

"He sure gets around. I met him briefly here. And where is he now, sir?"

"I believe he's in Europe somewhere, getting ready to fly. You're all right, Andrew. That's why I hired you."

Daniel's personal views on geopolitics were limited. He had read about the various summits between the United States and China, and the two nations appeared to him as friendly competitors. The official U.S. statements about China had been always designed to be friendly and accommodating. During the Taiwan oil crisis in the South Sea, the United States had responded relatively mildly even when the U.S. Navy was sent to "protect" Taiwan against China's clear aggression when its navy blockaded the Taiwanese port of Gaoxiong. The fact that the two countries had resolved their dispute at the Sydney Summit on New Year's Eve of 2040, and it had been reported to the entire world as a "peace treaty" between superpowers, made the American public more comfortable, especially when Chinese premier Mr. Wei declared, "Sometimes problems with brothers can make them closer."

So in the end, the American public, although aware of China's material supremacy, had not felt any serious or direct threat. Although Americans were jealous of China's continuing success and wealth, the average Chinese household income remained half of that in the United States. China did continue to own 50 percent of U.S. treasury bonds, but this had been proven the best remedy for peace. American economists reiterated the common view that America's best insurance policy for stability was the guarantee that China would not want to weaken its biggest customer.

Chinese public opinion was very different, however; the government had perfected the art of nationalism and had succeeded in building genuine support among its people. The Chinese government would never let good news go by without politicizing it and portraying it as a victory of the "mind of China" as opposed to the people of China. The nation appeared to have a supremacy complex; the people were set to prove their ascendancy on all levels and on every occasion.

The U.S. government had an altogether different take on the situation. After the government exhausted the soft-power approach that had succeeded in the first quarter of the twenty-first century, China became the unspoken enemy in the inner circles at all military, industrial, and technological levels. It was clear that the "enemy" had perfected espionage, especially when it came to intellectual property. During the Taiwan crisis, one general looked through his binoculars at the Chinese fleet and remarked, "They're replicas of *us*, goddamn them." This and similar incidents prompted Congress to increase the intelligence budget by 30 percent and to dedicate most of it to protecting U.S. assets and combating espionage from China while the U.S did its own spying. There had been major spy arrests at the U.S. Patent and Trademark Office and at the major weapon-design departments of Lockheed Martin and NASA. These, plus a recent arrest at Livermore Lab, appeared to have purged Chinese agents from these areas and dealt a severe blow to their intellectual-property spy rings. However, the Chinese were also good at cyber spying and soon would dispose of human help; their new *yīngxióng*, or heroes, would soon be on the job.

Daniel remained in a party mood, with no one on his case. He was enjoying every moment with Francesca, who introduced him to Indian food and showed him off to her Indian immigrant friends who called Italy home. He was impressed with her connections to the Indian embassy. She seemed to have friends in high positions in India, a remnant of the days when her father was part of the inner government circle there. Daniel asked Francesca to accompany him to China. Xi'an was a supporter of the CC, so Francesca felt she could find an excuse to go. Although the date for the interview was not yet set, Daniel's communication with Xi'an was cordial. The company offered him and a guest the cost of a first-class flight, and they even arranged for him to meet their "top and best scientists." Clearly they were setting the stage for a PR blitz.

The Chinese intelligence office at the Ministry of State Security (MSS) was privy to all communications between Xi'an and Daniel, as the company was partially owned by the Chinese government. The MSS was unable to crack the encrypted cloud service that Daniel was using, but they could see repeated and unsuccessful attempts to tag Daniel's Phonepad from the American side. These attempts began to increase at an alarming rate, a shocking development in the intelligence world and a sign of a high-priority target. The news quickly spread from the MSS to Xi'an that Daniel was potentially in danger; he was being tracked, and if the company needed to see him, it had to act immediately.

Daniel received a message stating that a Xi'an corporate jet in Rome was available for immediate use by him and a guest. The company requested that he "board immediately" so that he could confer with top Chinese Biological Investigators Society (CBIS) scientists meeting at the company headquarters. The conference was wrapping up—the following day would be its last—and Dr. Jenny Su, head of the society, was willing to wait for Daniel.

When Daniel read the message to Francesca, they were sitting in the middle of an unusually quiet *gelateria*, gazing at the Piazza di Spagna, and watching the typical commotion for which Rome was famous for. Their excitement was difficult to hide. Francesca had heard of Dr. Su. She explained that CBIS was a nonprofit organization that had similar goals to CC, and she hoped to get a tip or two by talking to Dr. Su. It was hard for Daniel to ignore the thrill of traveling on a private jet—an entire plane just for them.

"Let's go, *mio amante* (my love)," said Daniel. At that point a frantic John Masetti called. Daniel took the call but quickly blurted with a loud voice, "Let's talk in twelve hours or so, John. I am busy now, but in a great mood."

John did not know what to make of Daniel's remark. Felix had already chastised John for not following up on Daniel's moves, and now all John could do was simply report back that Daniel had agreed to talk in twelve hours.

Daniel and Francesca began to chase down a cab. They felt an immense sense of adventure, a rush that reminded them of the movie *Hanged*, which they had just seen.

"*Veloce* (fast), my darling," Daniel urged. While in the cab, Daniel replied to Xi'an: "We can be there in an hour. Please give us instructions on how to board."

Xi'an correspondent Ethan Lu was shocked. The bait had worked a little too well. He needed to procure a jet in Rome. Thanks to the Chinese embassy, it was hastily arranged on a moment's notice. A fictitious company made and paid for the reservation.

Private jet services had been around for over seventy years, and it was not difficult to hire a jet with an expensive price tag from a company called Jet Paradizo. It took about a half hour to get the details sent to Daniel. The message had excellent instructions for getting to gate P23 on the south end of Fiumicino, Leonardo da Vinci Airport. Ethan's next task was to find Dr. Su. A scramble to reach her at 3:30 a.m. was fruitless; she was in Sanya in South China, a common destination for winter vacations. But with the help of the MSS, she was not only awakened at five o'clock in the morning, in bed with her two daughters and husband by her side, but also briefed on Class 4 information (Class 4 was a code assigned to private citizens who were not told the entire story). She was told she would meet an American scientist and possibly his wife. He was the winner of a medal from the White House. His work was not known in detail, but Xi'an was hiring him, and it was important to paint the best possible picture so that he would stay. Dr. Su was to be in Xi'an within five hours on the pretext of a CBIS meeting, and she might see other scientists who had received the same orders. The reason for the hire was of highest security, and by the way, the government might recognize her "recruitment efforts" with a handsome donation to her organization, but time was of the essence.

It was a different story on the other side. The U.S. embassy in Rome had been notified through its resident intelligence officer, Mrs. Jacqueline Yolda, of the need to contact the Italian Servizio per le Informazioni e la Sicurezza Militare (SISMI, or Military Intelligence and Security Service) to arrest Daniel and take him to the embassy. The CIA's instructions, which she passed along to her Italian counterpart, specified that the arrest had to take place within six hours and had to be nonviolent arrest; the message read "give him a strong invitation to come to the embassy, leaving him no choice but to comply." Dr. Wu had been waiting at the private military wing of the embassy. He sat on a bright red sofa and interrupted his own deep sleep with violent snoring.

Italian drama was alive and well. When Officer Simone Lampondi received his instructions at about half past noon, he jumped on the occasion. He called his junior officers to an immediate briefing, at which he added that Daniel was a possible computer hacker as well as a scientist, and he was suspected to have stolen important secrets to sell. "We believe he is unarmed," advised Lampondi, "but we need to take precautions. He knows an Italian girl named Francesca Burbo that he might be with. Please leave her alone. Here's were he's staying, and here's his description."

He pressed a zap button on his Phonepad, and the entire file was transferred to his colleagues' Phonepads: photos, descriptions, and the place Daniel had last visited (according to his last PayGeo transaction at Gelato Uno on Piazza di Spagna about an hour earlier).

The officers split into three groups. One visited the gelateria, one went to Francesca's known address, and one stood by as a backup unit on the main circular highway, A91, one exit away from Fiumicino.

Daniel had been living out of his suitcase, but Francesca needed to pack for their trip to China. Daniel did his best to help her, and they finally stuffed a duffle bag with wheels on one end. Francesca was a frequent traveler but had never been inside a private jet. She was excited to fly in the high-speed plane that everyone talked about, although she hoped Daniel would ultimately settle in Rome. As the cab waited outside, it took them about six minutes to collect their clothes, shoes, and toiletries.

The unmarked car of SISMI agents pulled up to the apartment while Daniel and Francesca's cab took a turn at the end of the block and headed to the airport. As there was no search warrant, the agents waited for Officer Lampondi's instructions in the hallway while he tried in vain to get a forced-entry permit for search and seizure (his superior would deny the permit fifteen minutes later). The unit at the gelateria had been luckier. An employee who recognized the couple indicated that they had run away in a hurry, but he could not explain why.

The officers' next move was to call a general alert on all airports, trains, and seaports. Lampondi made the mistake of broadcasting on the carabinieri (Italian civilian police) channel that the officers should be on the lookout, with instructions to track but not detain Daniel, thus leaving the arrest to SISMI agents. As it turned out, the carabinieri used a relatively low-security digital frequency that was intercepted by the Chinese embassy. The message was relayed quickly, and there was a debate at the MSS headquarters as to whether the plan needed to be changed. The verdict was that an intelligence officer at the embassy should take two additional passports from their agents' inventory and rush to the airport's private terminal before Daniel could get there. The Chinese embassy was a grand property located at 56 Via Bruxelles on the edge of Villa Ada near the center of Rome. An ex–fighter pilot and motorbike champion named Jinlun was up to the task.

Jinlun grabbed the passports that most closely resembled Daniel and Francesca. Thanks to China's close relationship with the Federal Security Service (FSB) of Russia, the bogus passport holders happened to be from Lithuania, a noncontroversial country that had been off the international radar and thus was well suited to clandestine identities. The roads were hazardous, but Jinlun had to hurry. He took Via Ostiense, crossed the Tiber River at bullet speed (miraculously avoiding two collisions), took Highway A91 to Fiumicino, and reached Leonardo da Divinci Airport's gate P23 at the exact moment Daniel and his beautiful companion were getting out of their taxi.

Jinlun, who was handsome and athletic with a medium build, told Daniel and Francesca in a relaxed tone that he would accompany them on the trip. Insisting that they not show any documents to anyone before boarding the plane, he explained that he was their agent on the flight and had arranged for all the paperwork; they should proceed to the plane immediately.

The private terminal was lavish, and security was lax. However, after scanning their bags at the first security stop and before leaving the gated area, there was a passport control booth manned by an airport officer to ensure that all documents were scanned and in good order. Past the booth, a walkway led outside, where limos and private cars took passengers to the private planes parked on the edge of the runway.

Jinlun knew his way around. He waved his passengers through the gate, and before the Italian officer could get a good look at their faces, Jinlun handed him their new passports to scan—a common habit for VIP personnel and a familiar gesture to the officer. The couple still had no clue that they were being hunted; it was best that everything appear normal. The driver outside was given the plane's parking spot on his dashboard; he hardly looked behind him but did ask where they were going.

"America," Jinlun quickly replied, smiling at his guests. This was something Daniel did often—amuse himself with silly jokes on others. The pilot was obligated to have his passengers' names before taking off, but his company, Jet Paradizo, had a habit of delaying such information. This time it was the customer that was to blame: HM Industries, the fictitious company that operated within the Chinese embassy's walls, gave out the passengers' new names at the last minute—just as Andrius and Daina boarded the plane. The hostess was extremely friendly and happy to have such important guests. Knowing the cost involved, she presumed they were important executives.

Daniel wondered why the hostess greeted him in a foreign language and called him Andrius. "Why did she assume I can't speak English?" he thought. Francesca, now Daina, had a similar experience. Jinlun asked Daniel if he could sit near the front area by the cockpit, and Daniel agreed. This left the entire living room quarter, beside the private folding bed seats, for Daniel and Francesca. The plane was a twelve-person Gulfstream model X200, with an average speed near Mach 2 and a maximum range of 7,500 nautical miles. It had a leather interior, sleeping arrangements for four people, large folding screens at the corners, and a bright red Persian rug with a geometric design in the center. Daniel and Francesca were breathless to see such luxury; neither had seen anything like it.

The flight to Shenzhen was to take only about six hours. After the captain reported the usual information, such as distance and elevation, the plane began to move. A relieved Jinlun smiled and asked Daniel's permission to get a drink.

Daniel said, "You're the guest. You shouldn't be asking these questions. Please feel free to do whatever you'd like."

Francesca smiled and said, "It's your plane rather, we are the guests!"

Meanwhile, the Italian police had caught up with Jet Paradizo and found out that a flight carrying two Lithuanians and a Chinese man who fit the descriptions was about to take off. The police sent the private wing at the airport a general alert to stop the plane. The control tower radioed the pilot to abort takeoff if possible, but the reply was negative since he was about to lift off and had covered over two-thirds of the runway. The pilot said he would head back once he was at an altitude that would allow the plane to make a safe turn before landing again. The tower had given no explanation other than "Code S300," a conventional civil aviation security code alerting the pilot to a security breach. It was usually used during prison escapes or runaway incidents involving no weapons.

When Jinlun noticed a flight maneuver that was inconsistent with gaining altitude, he rushed to the cockpit and asked what was going on. The pilot responded that one of the plane's engines was showing erratic behavior, so it would be best to head back to the airport. Jinlun knew the protocol. He told the pilot in a gentle and firm manner that he himself was a pilot, and the original pilot should consider himself and the plane hijacked and refuse the control tower's request. Speaking in eloquent Italian and repeating himself, Jinlun added that if the pilot were to refuse, he would be risking his own life and that of everyone else on board.

"I am a Taiwanese Air Force pilot," Jinlun said. "Your two passengers have hired me to take over the plane and kill the pilot if necessary, although I prefer no bloodshed. I don't know much about my clients, except that they are wealthy heirs to a large corporation that I can't name."

The pilot, a young man in his mid thirties with rotating digital photos of his two-month-old daughter next to his chair, showed all signs of cooperation. He radioed back every detail Jinlun gave him, and the plane surged back to the northeast and headed toward the North Pole before descending to China on Earth's opposite side.

Full-speed travel meant that few military planes could catch up with this particular Gulfstream — and even if they could, the decision-making process would delay deployment and make it an unworthy attempt. The plane staff carried on with their normal routine. The news from Rome was hushed. No one from the public knew about this daring escape — not even the escapees themselves. It was a severe blow to Dr. Wu and his superiors, and a major disappointment to the Italian team. They had done everything possible to nab Daniel, but they were helpless when the plane was in the sky.

During the flight, Jinlun was busy on his Phonepad, using his access to one of China's secure satellites, to make sure that all tracks were covered. Another Chinese agent retrieved Jinlun's motorcycle and quietly made his way to the back door of the ambassador's residence. SISMI and their American agent did not know that neither fingerprints nor DNA could be retrieved from the bike; Chinese agents had been given the X treatment (Altering DNA), thanks to Xi'an's advanced technology.

There were some cool heads in the U.S. government. One was CIA director Mathew Cavers, who had been reviewing Daniel's file when Secretary Sheridan had asked for his opinion on what the Chinese would do if they were to bring Daniel's plane down. Mr. Cavers was alarmed that such a proposition was even being contemplated; he adamantly advised against the move and demanded to see the president.

The time allocated for the meeting was ten minutes. Mathew had failed to get more time from the chief of staff. Speaking in his characteristic southern drawl, he quickly got to the point. "Mr. President, I will make this short. I reviewed Dr. Oakley's file, and I think this administration is making a big mistake, sir. There is nothing here to suggest that this young man is up to no good. He's looking for a job in a good, old-fashioned manner, except *he's* the one interviewing the companies about what *they* have to offer. He's a hot commodity in his field and has been pampered here and there. From what I've heard, sir, there was talk about bringing his plane down — a *civilian* aircraft, sir —"

The president interrupted. "You've got it wrong here, Matt. I never authorized, and never would authorize, this kind of shenanigan, but this guy is a backstabber, and we want him here so that we can talk to him. I checked with Andrew, our chief counsel, and we have the full right to call this guy back here and talk to him and possibly let a civilian judge decide on the matter. It's all legal. I want him back here; there's too much at stake."

Mathew said, "Mr. President, I am very glad to hear that this idea of bringing the plane down — which I took to mean *shooting* it down — did not come from this office. I am honored to be working for a decent and levelheaded president. Now, about bringing him over. It would be best for him to come of his own free will, but I am worried that the Chinese won't let go of him, sir, and that soon he will be needing our help to get out of there. That's my take. Last thing, sir: there is a small possibility — I do mean a small one — that Dr. Oakley does not know what's going on around him."

"What do you mean?"

"Well, sir, the MSS can be very creative with how to snuff people. It wouldn't be the first time they snag someone. He could be drugged, misled . . . you name it, sir."

"What do you think we should do next, Matt?"

"Hang tight. Let our people on the ground over there tell us what's happening. Dr. Oakley is not an anarchist. No one in his family is cut from that cloth, sir. I think he's going to look around in Xi'an and see if he likes it or not."

President Lieberman said, "I am worried that he'll like it, stay there to work, and compromise whatever goddamned secrets we have left in this country."

"Sir, I am worried that he will *not* like it and will be prevented from leaving. That's what I think is likely to happen. His attorney is scheduled to talk to him tomorrow at about midnight our time, and he'll tell us what's going on."

Although the CIA had published its successes at catching spies and had advertised in style by hiring Hollywood directors to create ads best suited for action movies to boost its recruitment effort, this time the agency was counting on its top Chinese agent in Shenzhen. This individual named Jeff had a mixed record of violence and drinking, but he remained useful due to lack of alternatives. Two years earlier he had been credited with rightfully suspecting and tracking a colleague believed to be a double agent. Jeff was tenacious and vigorously pursued an associate spy, who had been lured into a freighter by another CIA agent posing to work for Russia, he was caught red handed trying to pass nuclear engine secrets to the 'Russians Navy' in exchange for 5 million Gs. That said, the pool of Chinese agents was large and reliable, and honest agents did exist. However the Dragon had been awakened, China will not be the same.

Chapter 7

The Leak: Titan out of the box

Daniel was awakened by the captain's announcement that they were about to land. He had been sleeping for over two hours. The plane was directed to land on a side runway normally used by military personnel or dignitaries visiting Shenzhen. They stepped outside to a crisp breeze. It was dark, and the local time was 1:05 a.m. Jinlun excused himself as soon as they exited the plane; it was the last time Daniel and Francesca would lay eyes on him. The couple was escorted to a parked limo that spirited them to the Dragon Inn, a medium-size, six-story hotel. It looked modern but had a signature Chinese curved roof with green tiles lit by LEDs that appeared to be built and wired inside each tile. It was an unusual sight.

Daniel's interview was set for 9 a.m. the following day at Xi'an's corporate headquarters. The couple had hardly slept when the screen by the bed lit up with a soft humming noise, indicating that the driver was downstairs waiting for them.

After going through several unmanned military checkpoints, Daniel and Francesca arrived at Xi'an's corporate offices within twenty minutes. The building was a medium-size glass high-rise shadowing large acres of land with multiple warehouses painted in bright blue. It looked impressive. The reception area was unusual. There was a single file of men and women, all dressed in white robes except for the first two men and one of the women — Dr. Su. Daniel and Francesca shook hands with each person and were shown the way to a waiting room next to a conference room at the end of the hall. Francesca was asked to sit on the sofa. After looking at Daniel, who replied with a concurring nod, she obliged. The conference room was filled with screens that covered the walls; from the ceiling, sophisticated cameras and sensors emitted soft blue lights. Daniel remarked that it looked like a newsroom. An artificial laugh followed as the general manager gave the signal for everyone to sit.

The general manager introduced himself as Dr. Ying and then presented the remaining five people at the table: Dr. Su and Dr. Tang, the only women; Dr. Zsu, dressed in white; and two men in suits, business development manager Dr. So and an MMS security officer named Mr. Mah, who was described as "our government liaison officer." Facing each chair was a tilted screen that read DR. DANIEL OAKLEY WELCOME MEETING. When the screen was touched, the offer letter that Daniel had received on February 13 appeared.

Dr. Tang made it known that she was the head of XNA studies, with an emphasis on zero-gravity experimentation. Daniel took an obvious interest in her introduction. Although he had planned not to reveal his emotions — he had been schooled in the basics of negotiation — it was against his nature to do so, and the experienced negotiators at the table took note of his vulnerability.

Dr. Ying, in a loud voice interrupted by an unnatural laugh, said, "Dr. Oakley, we want to welcome you to Xi'an and to our country, China. We are pleased that you have accepted our terms. . . . Not yet? Ha ha ha."

Daniel sensed that there was something wrong but could not put his finger on it. He had told Francesca on the plane that the whole Xi'an situation felt odd. He was trying to read everyone's body language, including the Italian pilot, who would never look Daniel in the eye when he left the plane on autopilot to step out and stretch. Everyone seemed to act as if they were being watched. Francesca kept disagreeing with Daniel. She'd say, "They're fine. They're just tired."

The conversation in the conference room seemed to be well rehearsed. Everyone talked except Mr. Mah. Dr. Tang pressed Daniel a bit on his fame. "Can you tell us why exactly you received the award from the president?" she asked.

"It was too generous of him," Daniel responded. "I don't think I deserved it myself. You have seen my published CV, correct?"

"Of course we saw it, but we would like to know more details if that is okay."

"Well, I researched 5hmC mutants to examine the roles of different genes in cognitive behavior. I isolated N-methyl-D-aspartate, receptors that play an important role in hippocampal . . ."

Daniel explained his research in a summary that he knew by heart.

Dr. Tsu said with a soft voice, "What is the new part about this, Dr. Oakley?"

"Well, I coated that 5hmC part that I know what it does on a charged silicon memristor."

"Very interesting, Dr. Oakley, but what does that do, anyway?"

Daniel looked at everyone around the table. He felt like a roasted bird on a plate, with hungry, large predator eyes all around. He knew he was talking too much, but he had to answer Dr. Tsu's question, so he went on describing the behaviors he had recorded and explaining how the results varied with different power sources. He was intent on boring his audience, but that did not work; they just kept soaking in the information.

Dr. Tang cut in at one point. "Then you look for the right area in the brain and use . . . what do you use?"

Daniel had grown pale and weak. He asked if he could have a glass of water. As he waited, his interviewers began to chat in Mandarin, and they smiled at him every time someone finished speaking. Meanwhile, Daniel wondered if there was any way to take charge of the interview.

Finally he was given a bottle of water and an empty glass cup printed with a large X with a globe in the middle. He thought it an odd symbol for Xi'an and couldn't help but think of the West's paranoia about Chinese world dominance. "This glass of water says a lot about what they are thinking," he thought.

Pretending that he felt way better than he did, Daniel was about to continue the meeting, but before he could say a word, Dr. Zsu suggested with a big smile that he let everyone read his patent. "Just zap it to the instrument on the table, and that way we won't bother you for too long today."

Daniel replied that he did not have the actual patent with him, but it was all in his head. Then, in a confident voice, he said, "I would like to see the zero-gravity lab, please, before we go on."

Dr. Ying replied with a more reserved tone. "Sure, Dr. Oakley, we can show you. Dr. Tang can take you . . . but you are not prepared for us? You should always carry important files, or at least be able to access them, when you travel, no?"

"Well, Dr. Ying, I think my government is paranoid. Maybe you can understand them, but I can't. They actually prevented me from ever cloudloading, downloading, or uploading the patent. Luckily, everything is up here." Daniel pointed to his head. "Crazy Americans, you know how they overreact"

"Okay, next subject," Dr. Ying said brusquely. Dr. Oakley, do you have any questions about our offer to work here?"

"I do. I want to see the facility where I would be working and the residence you offered. I want to learn more about the environment here. I also want to ask about vacations to go home and see my parents — details like that. If I recall, it is a yearly contract, and if I like the work and you still want me, I can renew, right?"

"Right, right. Of course. Okay, we have a lot of questions to answer. After lunch you will go with Dr. Tang to the zero lab and then come back here."

Dr. Ying got up, and everyone followed him as he made his way out of the room. Daniel caught Mr. Mah looking at his Phonepad.

"Very nice PP. Made in India?" Mr. Mah asked.

"No, I believe it's from Vietnam."

"They do very nice work there. Is this the PP8 or the PP10?"

Daniel said, "I think it's the 12."

"Ah, yes. So it can hold an entire database with many billions of records."

With that, Daniel knew he was doomed.

Mr. Mah believed that Daniel had his patents stored on his Phonepad — as well as Stanford's entire biomedical archive. A PP12 could access most clouds' algorithms and retrieve anything from anywhere, and if anything was viewed even once and then deleted, experts at the MSS were capable of retrieving data after everyone else had given up. All that would be unnecessary if the Chinese still had spies left at the USPTO, but for now it was best to play it safe. There would be plenty of opportunities for Xi'an to hack Daniel's Phonepad. Only a fool would refuse a job offer like the one Daniel had received.

Daniel reunited with Francesca, and they held hands as they took a company van to a fancy international restaurant whose chefs were talented at replicating authentic dishes from all over the globe.

A call from John appeared on Daniel's Phonepad. He walked out to the lobby to answer it, but when he noticed all the blue sensor lights above him, he knew that he was being watched and that his conversation would probably not be private. Daniel stepped outside in the cold and had a short conversation with his attorney. He reported that he was in China and that in the evening he would write John a note telling him all about it. John said he needed to know if Daniel was staying there, but Daniel just said, "I don't know yet."

Then, to Daniel's surprise, John said, "Everyone is looking for you."

"Who is looking for me, and why?"

"Well, Daniel, you're not suppose to be in China. It doesn't make sense. Don't you love your country?"

Upset that John was questioning his patriotism, Daniel lashed out. "I am doing what I want to do, and everyone else should do the same. I love my country, and if I don't like it here, I will leave. I will write to you later in the evening."

Outside the restaurant, Xi'an's sensors transmitted Daniel's conversation via security interlinks to Dr. Ying, who was debating with Mr. Mah about what to do with Daniel in the event that he refused Xi'an's job offer. The conversation centered on defining priorities. Daniel's employment, plus an amicable arrangement to share his patent, would be the ultimate goal. Short of that, access to Daniel's patent was a second option. Under no circumstances, however, should Xi'an waste its efforts to lure Daniel and let him leave for nothing.

Daniel's comment to John about loving his country was very disturbing. It meant that one day Daniel's need to prove his loyalty could very well turn him into a spy. Dr. Ying and Mr. Mah were disgusted that Daniel would make such a comment about the United States. They had been taught that Americans were not patriotic—they hardly participated in their own elections, and the only motivation for them to serve in the armed forces was money. It seemed Daniel had proved them wrong—for a moment, at least. They laid the debate to rest after agreeing that Daniel was a special case; the president had corrupted his mind by awarding him a medal. Regardless, no one who loved the U.S. ought to work within the walls of Xi'an—or anywhere in China, for that matter.

Dr. Ying asked, "What if Daniel was lying on that call? What if he does not love America?"

Mr. Mah replied, "He's an amateur. I've been taught to read people, and Daniel is telling the truth. The boy could be dangerous here."

Mr. Mah concluded that it would be best just to get the patent. "Let's have our own brilliant minds look at it," he said. "I guarantee they will outsmart this American child and produce better results. There are plenty of ways to 'transfer' the patent—by force or by intelligence—but the best is the old-fashioned fake robbery. It's the cleanest technique, and it gives us the necessary time to hack his machine."

After lunch, Dr. Ying did not bother returning to the conference room. Instead, Mr. Mah apologized on his behalf and explained that there was an emergency situation Dr. Ying had to cover. Daniel was relieved, but he noticed that everyone at the table became more casual. The interviewers began to ask him questions about topics that were not related to his employment—movies he liked, books he read, pets, and so on. Mr. Mah talked about his love of birds and how much he studied them. Dr. Su remarked that she had enjoyed talking to Daniel's friend Francesca and that she would love to invite them over for dinner after they left Xi'an.

As it turned out, everyone had recognized the signal from Dr. Ying and the wink from Mr. Mah: no show meant no hire.

Daniel, feeling a pleasant change in the atmosphere, began having second thoughts about his initial reaction. What if he *could* work for these guys? After all, they seemed pleasant now, and maybe it was just a matter of time to get used to them. While watching the relieved faces of the group, he began speculating that they were under severe pressure to perform their duties. Surely it was common to show respect to the boss while he was present, but this had been different. He thought, "Could it be that they are freedom-loving people like me but have not had a chance to express it?"

The reality was a combination of many elements. The Xi'an employees knew that the interview no longer mattered; they would never again see Daniel and his companion. There was also a kernel of truth to Daniel's speculation: Dr. Ying was an autocrat hired by the government to head Xi'an with absolute authority. He demanded blind dedication but was privately detested by employees. Their nonscientific questions to Daniel allowed them a glimpse of life outside their world. China, although open compared to recent standards, was far from being free. Prying into the daily life of an American scientist was an opportunity to gauge if they were working in a repressive atmosphere compared to that of their parents.

Dr. Su invited Daniel, Francesca, and Dr. Tang to dinner at an Italian restaurant called Marco Chino, a reference to Marco Polo's twelfth-century visit to China. According to legend, after living in China for seventeen years, Polo brought pasta-making techniques home to Italy. Daniel asked Francesca to tuck his Phonepad in her purse. He had seen the look on Mr. Mah's face, and the thought of having his device stolen and hacked had crossed his mind. The second part of the interview had relieved his suspicion, however, and he had remarked to Francesca, "These guys could do no evil."

John sent a note to Felix at the HMD office after his short conversation with Daniel. He wrote, "Daniel does not seem aware that he was being followed, or that he was on a hijacked plane. I was promised a note from him in the evening, which means the early hours PST tomorrow. I will forward it immediately for your review."

The news reached the CIA office, and agents immediately sprang to action. It looked like Mathew Cavers, head of the CIA, had been correct in his assessment of the situation. The mobilized agents included Dr. Su, who had just reported on her hasty trip to Xi'an and had contributed invaluable data on other facilities as well. In return for her services, the CIA would donate money to the CBIS through fictitious grants from the United States, a small price to pay for her help with vital cases. Being the head of CBIS afforded Dr. Su opportunities to meet with people in top positions of authority. The methods used to organize her communications with the CIA were atypical and included two media platforms. One involved hacking her "memoir," which contained details that were not urgent. The second involved exchanging files and instructions that appeared to be neutral comments on fake book-club websites set up by agent "authors." The memoirs, which would be written every evening or when possible, were to include everyday topics mixed with the critical part that the CIA could easily decipher. There were occasions when a CIA agent acting as one of the "donors" to her organization would ask for a meeting to review "progress" on the funds invested in her various charitable programs.

All should appear innocent and with no solid evidence that the agent had meant harm to his or her country. Dr. Su had been trained every time she met with her "donors," and she had become satisfied with the arrangements. She had become a veteran by now, having been recruited in Italy at the ninety-ninth NATO conference on April 20. The MSS had attempted to recruit her as well; seeing the access granted to her organization, the ministry's leaders felt the same need to take advantage of it. Mr. Mah had been the driving force behind recruiting Dr. Su. At the time, she had "confided" in him that she did not want to burden her family with official "projects"; instead, she preferred to continue helping needy children. For now Xi'an would leave Dr. Su alone. Mr. Mah had CBIS covered with Dr. Su's personal assistant Juliette, the accountant officer of the MSS.

While on the plane to China, Dr. Su had written in her "memoir" about the sudden urgency requiring her to be at Xi'an, so the CIA knew the entire setup well ahead of Daniel. Dr. Su's update would have to wait until later in the evening. However, while she was waiting for her guests at Marco Chino, she was able to write, "Today the American recruit was fooled . . . Xi'an will not hire him . . . not sure of the reason . . . maybe they will tell me later."

Suddenly a perturbed Daniel and Francesca showed up. "We've been robbed!" Daniel cried. "Dr. Su, I need to log on to your Phonepad. I need to kill my own PP."

"Oh, I'm so sorry, Daniel! I can't have you use mine. Use the tablet at the entrance. It's open to the public. What happened?"

Daniel ran to the front reception area, where tablets were mounted on the walls. They looked like picture frames but were actually interactive computers that guests at the restaurant could access for free. He managed to log on to his secure cloud, and within less than a minute he was able to activate the kill command.

Francesca had a blank look on her face. She explained that someone had grabbed her purse, which contained both PPs, just as she was exiting their taxi. Daniel returned to the table. He felt relieved to have blocked access to his machine, and he asked Francesca to do the same. He was upset that their taxi driver had refused to pursue the thieves on their motorcycle, but then he realized how futile it would have been.

Daniel begged Dr. Su to forgo dinner and take them to an Estoria (a Chinese electronics store) instead so that they could purchase new PPs and re-access the money and information saved on their cloud accounts. Dr. Su agreed and called the local police while they rode in the cab.

The MSS agents managed to beat Daniel and download every bit of information from his Phonepad within less than a minute; one agent had driven the motorcycle while the other had used a state-of-the-art USX with 328 TG of memory. This meant that in a matter of hours they would find out all the details — patent documents, reports, private conversations, PayGeo account locations, and, ultimately, the key to his heart: did Daniel really love his country?

Dr. Su managed to post more encrypted information for her CIA contact, this time in the form of a comment on an interactive novel on a website called Cloudbook: "The man deserves to lose all his possessions for the terrible deed . . . he should start looking for help." These words meant Daniel had already lost his possessions and needed help.

A swift reply from another "reader" asked, "What do you propose to rehabilitate character and shelter?"

"I will think about it and provide you an answer," she replied.

Dr. Su called Juliette to ask for her family's address, she knew she had been born there and lived in the neighborhood for most of her life. Juliette wasted no time reporting Dr. Su's question to Mr. Mah, who advised her to give Dr. Su a new address for an apartment that was used by the MSS agents. Mr. Mah became very suspicious and asked his team to try and hack Dr. Su's PP. The agents reported that Dr. Su had a habit of commenting on book-club websites, and her personal journal contained a lot of information jumbled with other comments about food, books, and ordinary family stuff. The journal had poor security and was likely viewed by others. This was enough evidence for the seasoned officer to conclude that Dr. Su had been deceiving him for all these years and deserved no mercy.

In the meantime, minutes before the second round of meetings at Xi'an the following morning, Dr. Su was able to pass on to Daniel a "safe" address that she directed him to use in case of emergency. Mr. Mah's agents working in Xi'an had detected this message and alerted him just before he headed to the meeting. He tried to control his anger as he entered the conference room.

"Let's do a tour of the zero lab for Daniel. Please, this way. Follow me."

Mr. Mah made eye contact with no one. He proceeded to the van outside and asked the driver to go to Building 13. Dr. Tang wondered why he had asked to go to the wrong building—the zero lab was located in Building 43—but she had learned not to question such matters. Mr. Mah told his guests that he wanted to show them a collection of birds. Xi'an provided vaccines to fight bird diseases, thus keeping them from going extinct. It was a fascinating place, with large cages built in framed aluminum with thick glass windows and doors suited more to vaults rather than to a lab environment. The birds were exotic creatures gathered from all over the word. Some doors had skull-and-crossbones signs, some had a sun symbol, and others had a water symbol. All doors were marked with

Chinese characters as well presumably relating to the content inside or the type of testing taking place in these rooms.

The young lady at reception was leading the way. Directing them toward the end of the corridor, she asked them to feel free to look through all the windows but not to go inside the large cages. Mr. Mah had whispered to Dr. Su to come closer, and right when she turned the corner, he grabbed her left hand, opened the adjacent door, ushered her in, and asked her to wait for him.

The room had a strange smell that resembled a pesticide. There were four large plants in one corner, and one wall had empty cylindrical holes with Plexiglas windows that began to open one by one. There were no chairs. Dr. Su wondered, "What could Mr. Mah want, and why here?"

Birds began to appear in the cylinders. She knew they were known as *tsitzi*, or sparrow hawks. They began flying toward the plants at the back of the room. More and more hawks appeared — twenty, then thirty, then a hundred. They all faced Dr. Su, who began to get worried. She tried to leave, but the door was locked. She began to panic, even before the birds showed any sign of hostility. Dr. Su started slamming windows and pushing buttons on the wall in a desperate attempt to get someone to open the door.

The birds that Mr. Mah enjoyed so much were the result of multiple processes, including forced genetic drift, also known as genetic hitchhiking, whereby scientists isolated a genetic mutation in a particular predator and multiplied it beyond its natural evolutionary variation. It resulted in aggressive behavior and an amplified hunting instinct in animals that could be used as deadly weapons.

Dr. Su met her end in the most horrific way. The birds flocked to her as if they were obeying a command. As she tried to hide her eyes from their sharp beaks, they ripped apart her elbows and then covered her entire body. Overwhelmed by the uncontrollable beasts, Dr. Su fell on the floor, where the birds ravaged every last bit of her flesh. It was a ghastly sight, as the hawks crowded together and fought for their meal on top of her lifeless body.

Chinese sparrow hawk

Mr. Mah did not go back to see the results of his deed; the crime scene was left for others to clean up. Instead, in a cold and calm manner, he continued to guide the group past the various cages. They walked along the entire hallway at the perimeter of the room before making their way back to the entrance. The van remained outside. Daniel asked about Dr. Su's whereabouts, and Mr. Mah replied that she had gotten an important call and needed to leave, but she would probably show up for lunch.

When they reached the zero lab, Daniel noticed Mr. Mah speaking to Dr. Tang in a reprimanding way. Although he could not understand the conversation, he could sense a degree of agitation that left her looking troubled. The visit was surprisingly short. Daniel was not allowed beyond the large glass window at the front of the lab, and for safety reasons he needed to go through the conditioning vacuum room. That would take a lot of time which they did not have as explained by Dr. Zsu.

Mr. Mah was showing some signs of regret about killing Dr. Su. He was irritable and loud, and everyone avoided him. Dr. Su's betrayal had made him suspicious of everyone. Had he not taken the matter into his own hands, the military court would have taken over, and Dr. Su would have suffered years in harsh prison conditions before meeting the death squad. Mr. Mah would probably not be chastised for disposing of her himself; he held a high position and had friends in all branches of government. The only reprimand he would receive would be his own conscience, punishing him for taking the life of a mother in her prime without knowing or caring to find out the circumstances that led her to become a spy.

Mathew Cavers saw Dr. Su's report in the early hours of Daniel's second day in China. He was furious that his order to mobilize agents had not been taken seriously by the CIA operation desk. He rebuked the intellectual intelligence manager and asked him to stop the CIA agents from making any precarious moves that could be detected. Then he called the secretary of state and asked to have the U.S. ambassador to China intervene to find out Daniel's whereabouts, to demand that Chinese intelligence officers facilitate his moves in the country, and to have him meet a member of the U.S. embassy staff immediately.

Mathew's reasoning was that, once the Chinese government and the MSS were officially notified that Daniel was indeed in China and the public learned that the United States was concerned about its scientist, the Chinese would have no choice but to confirm his presence and turn him over. Mathew suggested that the secretary of state run this proposal by the president and explain that underground solutions to problems of this sort could backfire by exposing covert agents, in addition to endangering the lives of everyone involved. The fact that the Chinese agents had managed to snitch Daniel and fly him to China on a private plane was not a transgression by itself; it could be challenged, as it appeared Daniel went of his own free will. The U.S. government's only official concern would be his safety — nothing else.

At Xi'an the tension was building. Staff and security services showed up in droves while security officials can only be heard saying *yìwài* (accident) Ambulances came and went in the lobby. The atmosphere had shifted, and anxiety was on everyone's face. Mr. Mah, with his shifty eyes and rude manner, indicated to Daniel that it was "not good to continue" with the interview today because there was an "emergency situation." He told Daniel to go back to his hotel room and await a message detailing next steps.

It was a bizarre turnaround from the previous day; no one had paid special attention to Daniel or said anything scientifically meaningful. It appeared that a real emergency was at hand. Daniel kept looking through the window on his ride back to the hotel. He half expected to see a cloud of smoke or something else that could explain the uproar.

Francesca attempted to reach Dr. Su but failed. It was a long night; Daniel and Francesca hardly slept. In the early morning hours, they noticed a yellow envelope slip under the door. It was a letter from Xi'an requesting that Daniel immediately call the U.S. consulate and advising him that there was "no need for further discussion at Xi'an's headquarters," but they would be contacting him at a later date to follow up on the discussions they had already had. At the bottom of the page was a reservation code number on Cathay Airlines, along with instructions to "use this to validate your trip to Rome."

Xi'an had gotten what they wanted: all the technical knowledge to build Titan, as well as plenty of personal and financial information about Daniel. It was clear that his heart was in the United States; Xi'an's leaders had counted forty-eight uses of the phrase "I love my country" in Daniel's communications to friends, relatives, and even his attorney. Xi'an could not afford someone like that working in their midst.

Daniel answered a call from John. He told his lawyer that he had been robbed, but that his PP had not been compromised because he had managed to kill the data. Daniel added that he and Francesca would be taking a quick tour of Shenzhen before heading back to Rome and that it was unlikely that he would work at Xi'an. Finally, he told John about the letter directing him to contact the U.S. embassy and said that his initial inclination was not to bother replying. John begged Daniel to comply. "This could be serious," he said. "You may have been reported as a missing person, Daniel."

The Chinese government seemed to be cooperating with the U.S. government's demands. On behalf of the MSS, Dr. Ying wrote a statement reporting that Daniel had been interviewed for a scientist position at Xi'an but, regrettably, had not met the company's standards. The statement was deliberately given to the U.S.

ambassador, Karen Kuvek, in order to infuriate the Americans by suggesting that their medal-winning scientist was ranked below his average Chinese equivalent.

The MSS leaked the news to the English- language *China Times* media, and the newswire was flooded with headlines such as "U.S. Top Scientist Fails Xi'an Test" and "U.S. Medal-Winning Scientist Under qualified." Soon Daniel received a call from his dad, wondering where he was and asking him about the rumors that were beginning to circulate through the U.S. news outlets. "What's this about you not passing an exam, son?" he asked.

Daniel was furious. He explained to his dad that the stories were lies. No such exam existed, and he suspected someone was trying to destroy his reputation — either Xi'an or the folks over at Livermore. Robert begged his son to come home, while at the same time assuring him that he had not reported Daniel missing. However, Daniel avoided committing to any specific return date.

The Chinese government continued to manipulate the situation. While Daniel was having a late breakfast with Francesca at his hotel, a commando unit with three men and one woman surprised them at the table and demanded they accompany them to the U.S. embassy. They claimed it was an official request by the U.S. government, and they could use force if necessary. Francesca assumed they were only talking about Daniel, but she was wrong; the elite woman soldier barked, "All together." The soldiers followed the couple to their room, waited for them to pack, escorted them to a modern, Chinese-made SUV, and whisked them through the wide boulevards with unusual speed.

The soldiers ignored Daniel's repeated questions and instructed him and Francesca not to talk. Daniel was furious. He attempted to reach the embassy, but one of the commandos ordered him not to use his PP. Daniel knew that the embassy was located in Beijing, approximately 1,200 miles away, but he hoped they would be taken to the consulate general in Guangzhou, just 20 miles away.

Daniel was correct about their destination. At the front gate of the consulate stood a U.S. marine who saluted the couple when they were dropped off. One of the Chinese commandos tossed Francesca's duffle bag on the sidewalk with derision and intentional disrespect. Daniel was lucky to see the ambassador, who was waiting for him at the consulate. Karen Kuvek was a gentle, intelligent woman who had been raised in Southern California and knew all too well the dynamics of college students and their need to make their mark after graduation; she had been the UC's (University of California) International relation coordinator for 20 years. She tried to calm Daniel down and explained how dangerous small matters could become — a silly job interview had gotten out of control and had required government intervention to ensure his safety. He requested that the embassy issue a communiqué refuting the Chinese version of his "failing the test." She promised to check with the U.S. State Department before sending out a press release, but for the time being she felt she was lucky to see Daniel alive and well. She asked why his passport had not been stamped with a Chinese entry visa. Daniel had no answer except that they had chartered a private plane and that the omission was probably intentional for some reason only Xi'an would know.

The news that Daniel was within the U.S's embassy compound was welcomed at the CIA headquarters, but soon they realized that smearing Dr. Oakley in the Chinese media, while the story was copied and repeated by the rest of the world news outlets, had been deliberate. It was not a goodwill gesture, as China's politicians had suggested; instead they apparently had gotten what they wanted — Daniel's patent secret — and realized he was no longer needed. They would not have given him up so easily had they wanted any more information; *compassion* was not a word in the MSS's dictionary.

What the CIA did not know was that Mr. Mah himself was a double agent working for the FSB. The Chinese and the Russians shared a historical disdain for the United States, so they exchanged intelligence and hid each other's agents when desirable. Mr. Mah relayed the entire Daniel Oakley situation to his Russian counterpart and friend, who resided in Shenzhen, over a few beers. "My MSS team retrieved the entire Titan patent within less than a minute," Mr. Mah bragged.

Later in the conversation, after his third beer, Mr. Mah remarked, "Don't ask me if I can pass on the patent to your people. I would need authorization, and that I may never get."

His friend Caspar Vildaof understood very well that this time around, money would talk. He knew Mr. Mah well—they had been friends for over eight years—and although Mr. Mah was intelligent, he had vulnerability to alcohol that did not agree with his impulsive nature. He hated losing bets and Caspar had fudged a loss many times to keep him happy. His worst reaction to date occurred when he lost a chess game and flipped the board onto his Caspar's head . . . and that was the last time Mr. Mah lost a chess game. Caspar found Mr. Mah too valuable to let his own ego get in the way, so he accommodated the Chinese agent. Time and again Caspar commented on how smart Mr. Mah was— a guarantee to stay on his good side. He also knew that Mr. Mah was extremely attached to his granddaughter; Mr. Mah would always play silly videos proving to Caspar how smart and articulate a two- , three-, and six-year-old could be. Mr. Mah dearly wished that after he died, his granddaughter would be financially secure for life. Her parents were university teachers and had not been able to garner fortunes like Dr. Su—a name that Mr. Mah kept repeating to Caspar, suggesting that he was either truly impressed with her, jealous of her, or bot. She was an attractive woman, and that may have added to his confusion.

After the FSB helped the Chinese with the passport exchange favor in Rome, Caspar alerted his superior in Moscow that something of great importance was going on. The Russians had their satellite tracking Jinlun on the motorcycle and, later on, the flight pattern of his guests, and they listened to the pilot's conversation without making a definitive assessment of the situation. When Caspar cleared up the entire operation story of how the Chinese had managed to get Daniel's patent, they were very impressed, and they agreed to deposit, through a fictitious stock-trading house, one million G on a PayGeo account in Mr. Mah's granddaughter's name. The following evening at the bar, Caspar was told that the gift had been transferred, and he handed Mr. Mah a beer napkin with an account number and a password written on the back. It took Mr. Mah less than a minute to pass the entire Titan file to Caspar. Then they spent the rest of the evening talking about Mr. Mah's heroic dealings with American and Japanese secret agents.

Back at the consulate, Ambassador Kuvek chastised Daniel for causing political tension when he would not heed good advice not to come to China. She questioned the media reports about Xi'an's employment exam, and he assured her that it had been a fabrication. She said, "I believe you. At the same time, you must remember how brutal certain companies are. Their governments back them up if it is in their best interest to smear someone. Who do you think benefits from thrashing your name?"

Daniel did not have a good answer. "I think they sensed that I was going to refuse their offer and wanted to simply protect their ego," he said.

In reality, after confirming that he was a "U.S. sympathizer" and thus unsuitable for the job, and after hacking all of Titan's technical specs, Xi'an viewed Daniel as dispensable and intended to assassinate him. It would be a staged accident that included sacrificing innocent civilians, such as a private pilot, one flight attendant, and Francesca. The Cathay Pacific itinerary that Xi'an had left at Daniel's hotel contained encoded instructions for security personnel to take Daniel and his friend to a private terminal. There, the couple would have entered a small plane rigged by special agents to explode at an altitude of four thousand feet. Thanks to the CIA director, however, the plan had been thwarted, and bloodshed had been averted this time. In addition, the news of Daniel's presence at Xi'an had been made public, thus forcing the Chinese to acknowledge his existence. This had been another blow to the MSS's plan.

In retaliation, the MSS chose to stain Daniel's reputation and undermine his marketability with the bogus story about Xi'an's employment test. This would give them a head start on studying their heist and potentially developing Titan.

For now the ambassador was satisfied that there had been no breach of patent information. She asked Daniel to take a flight to San Francisco the following day. He hesitated, and she gave him a stern warning. "You are under no obligation to obey, Dr. Oakley, but let's be clear: if you walk out of this building, your life may be in jeopardy. The Chinese are watching us — our security here can tell that you're under surveillance. It's your call. Walk out to the wolves, or go home to your country and get treated with respect."

"I am not questioning that, ambassador — I don't like their manners one bit — but I'd like to go back to Rome instead. Is that possible?"

"No, go to San Francisco first, and then do what you want."

Daniel turned to Francesca, who seemed to agree. She asked to make a phone call to a friend named Aab, an Indian expatriate currently working with a local NGO. Aab was happy to hear from Francesca, who asked her if she could spend a few more days in Shenzhen. Francesca decided to stay, as she was not part of this affair. She would join Daniel later.

Francesca told Aab about her new love and gave her a glimpse of the Titan project. Aab begged Francesca to introduce Daniel to her cousin Sunny, who worked for an Indian biomedical company called Gauv Bio. Thanks to a dedicated budget for outside discoveries, the company would have a good position for Daniel. Sunny traveled to the United States frequently, and Aab hoped they all could connect.

Chapter 8

The Race to Be Superhuman

It did not take long for Sunny to make contact with Francesca, who agreed to bring Daniel to a local café in Burlingame. They had an intense, two-hour conversation about Titan. Sunny listened to the overview but and then asked for a copy of the patent so that he could study the invention further. Although Sunny seemed like an honest person, Daniel politely declined. "It's a work in progress," he explained.

Sunny offered Daniel Guav Bio's facility to continue working on Titan and reminded him that the first commercial zero-gravity lab had been installed there. Daniel said that once he cleared up his obligation to the United States, he would be on the move again. He admitted that Respi had seemed to be the best place so far, but he did not mention the elephant in the room — the U.S. government. John Massetti was still on Daniel's case to sign the second-draft employment letter, to visit Livermore for his official interview with Dr. Wu — ultimately, to keep his promise to the president.

Daniel admitted to Francesca that he was afraid he would be stuck in the United States — "They might prevent me from traveling for security reasons," he pointed out. John had hinted that the U.S. government could choose that route, but Daniel could not get a straight answer about its legality. Overall, Daniel was afraid to work at any firm that was connected to the military, as he feared the worst: Titan's development could take a dangerous course if it were "deployed" on healthy individuals. In an "on-demand" environment, the memristor could be programmed to boost any particular function — physical or motor enhancement could create superathletes, while intellectual enhancement could yield superscientists. Daniel wanted his patent to fall in the right hands — in the hands of people who would guarantee Titan's use with kids who suffered on a daily basis due to their disabilities.

Daniel asked Francesca to stay with him in California if he ended up working at Livermore, a thought he disdained. He then promised her that he would eventually join the right company, where the atmosphere was free of "evil thoughts" and scientists were working for the betterment of humanity's weakest. He dreamed of working anonymously in Egypt and wondered if there were any advanced companies with sophisticated laboratories there. These were romantic thoughts, not common to scientists.

Sunny starting lobbying his cousin Aab to obtain the Titan patent. Aab repeatedly spoke with Francesca and somehow elicited details about Daniel's anxieties. With a stroke of luck, Francesca was the one who initiated the idea to pass the patent along to Sunny. "Daniel will not be mad if Sunny's company is as truthful as he says it is," Francesca claimed. "He will not mind. He liked Sunny."

Aab delicately confirmed the good nature of both Sunny and his company. She told Francesca about the many yearly donations the company made to the needy, as well as the free medicine they administered to children.

"Daniel will not regret it," Aab assured her. "He will proud."

The Russians, like their Chinese counterparts, wasted no time exploring the data passed on by Mr. Mah. A special unit at Military Moscow Biomedical University was charged with reading, duplicating, and improving on the Titan. In two distant countries the race had begun on a project that the United States had tried in vain to keep a lid on. The Americans simply had not been able to keep their scientist in check. The governments of these two distant countries shared ill will toward America, a competitive complex, and a blind need to prove their superiority, both to the world and to their own people. Daniel's findings soon would be shown on the world stage, each country taking credit for its own scientific supremacy and proving it in ways that would amaze everyone — while simultaneously shaming the United States. No one could be blamed for this turn of events except Daniel Oakley himself. His ego had created a potential disaster of international proportions.

The Russians soon used Titan on healthy individuals. Their scientists harnessed well-studied areas of the brain to power memristor 5hmC with layers of encyclopedic knowledge on silicon chips. They utilized photovoltaic implants that generated power wirelessly — just as Daniel had done at Stanford — and sent infrared beams straight to the underperformed area of the animal brains. Through this process they created superhumans with a previously inconceivable capacity to analyze experimental data, thus yielding results that would have taken normal scientists decades. On newswires the Russians were conspicuously shown allowing world scientists and reporters a short opportunity to test for themselves this new breed of superhumans. Meanwhile, U.S. agents on the ground lacked the high level agent-office penetrations they had enjoyed for years, as a recent purge had made their lower-level intelligence sketchy and unreliable.

The first shock of the Russians' might came at the Warsaw World Biophysics Conference less than six months after Mr. Mah leaked Daniel's patent. The Russians had promised a surprise fifteen-minute press conference, whose attendees would be invited to pose any question they wanted to the Titan superscientist. This would prove to the world the advanced intellectual stage Russia had reached. These questions, which involved extremely complex numbers and algorithms, were posed to four well-dressed people with model-grade physiques. The superscientists answered with shocking speed and eloquence that left everyone awestruck.

During the short news conference, the superscientists — two women and two men — predicted the appearance of the next nuclear fusion engine, which would take humans to Mars. They provided complex details that the crowd could not possibly fathom, until the FSB finally stopped them from overexposing projects they were working on. The official claim was that these superscientists, and many more like them, owed their success to the excellent Russian educational system, which made it possible to develop and display such talent.

At the domestic level, Russian news releases would extol the uniqueness of the Russian people and their legacy of winning historic battles, building great empires, and demonstrating an unmatched capacity for learning. It was reminiscent of the Nazis' Aryan propaganda nearly a century earlier. The Russian public felt a euphoric nationalism that was hard to contain, as the government continued to parade superhumans with extraordinary skills that were hard to explain. This new phenomenon inspired a serious debate among the people. They wondered unashamedly how many super-Russians the country would need before they could rule the world.

Americans took notice. The American people guessed that the superscientists had to be artificial, yet they secretly admired the individuals that seemed so abundant in Russia. It would take none other than the head of the CIA, Mathew Cavers, to figure out that these were the effects of Titan at work . . . and something had to be done *fast*.

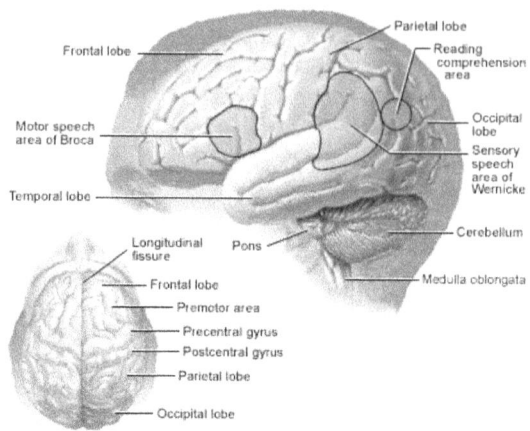

The fact that Russian scientists working for the FSB were themselves being administered the "Titan treatment" would be the FSB's own undoing. The newly graduated and "treated" elites would quickly turn against the system that allowed them this superior mental power. Claiming that they had a solemn duty to do more for their nation, they formed the поборник Club, translated as the Apostle Club. This group had two main goals. First, they swore to protect Russia by using their improved capacity to predict future drugs, treatments, technology, economic trends, and so on. Second, they sought to be the driving ruling force in the government — the "new Bolsheviks," watching overzealous politicians and making better decisions for the nation. They saw themselves as the chosen ones, who were beyond corruption. "What's best is what's best for Russia" was their credo — eerily similar to Hitler's "What's good is what's good for Germany." Amazingly, the Apostles were not concerned about how this mode of thinking had brought devastation to Germany and Russia.

It did not take long for China to show its own superscientists. Unlike the Russians, the Chinese chose not to parade them on the international scene. Instead, they organized appearances in close academic circles comprised of only Chinese. The enhanced individuals, known as the *yīngxióng* ("heroes"), held court on an extensive list of matters that were not open for discussion in public. For example, the "heroes" would appear at medical facilities and universities to train staff on new methods they had discovered, thus shortening the learning curve. The government allowed only Xi'an to produce "heroes." The company's zero-gravity lab had enhanced the XNA mutation with 5hmC that was layered over silicon memory chips, allowing for faster and more robust materials capable of being slipped under the skin and over the skull, with nanowires inserted in the part of the brain that was to be enhanced. It was just as Daniel had predicted.

The Chinese devoted significant efforts to the motor area of the cortex, as the government wanted to create superathletes to compete in world sports events like soccer. They would implant Titan in team members favored by certain politicians, sometimes without the athletes' knowledge. The Chinese international soccer team began to dominate its rivals; occasionally it would allow a loss, mostly for the sake of disguise. These clever implants would go undetected, as they greatly exceeded the effects of the sophisticated steroids that other international teams commonly used. Sometimes it was necessary for the athletes to undergo a second or third Titan chip implant as competition extended to their own. As a result, China created superstars who packed stadiums everywhere, and soon there was an internal race to "retrofit" players, even at the national level.

About a month after the theft of Daniel's patent, the Chinese government began building a new facility at Xi'an. Designed by one of the "heroes," it would accommodate research and development, mostly on the XNA memristor. U.S. agents transmitted an unusual increase in activities and communications between Xi'an and the MSS. All of the agents except one suggested that a secret biophysical weapon was being developed. The sole objector and newest recruit, Dr. So, the business development manager at Xi'an, suggested that the company was doing a study on human brains. Xi'an liberally installed Titans with new intellectual-enhancement chips in scientists from various fields. Not every installment was successful; there were reported deaths with causes that were not fully understood. There were so-called rigor screenings that provided better life expectancy for the "heroes"; however, political goals would continue to supersede the scientific method, and the program remained plagued with unexplained loss of life.

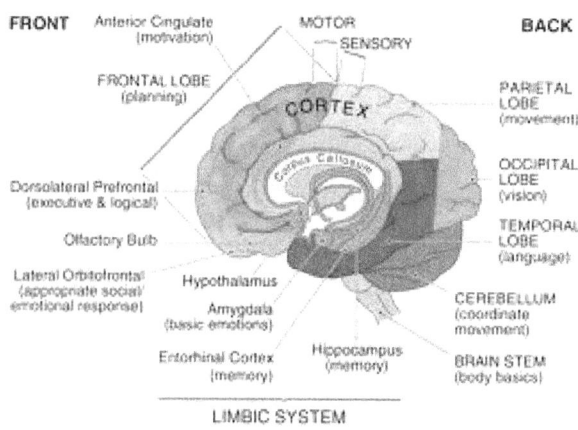

It had been four months since Daniel had agreed to work at Livermore. The new phase of his life and work had started surprisingly well. He had moved to Danville and found a lavish home to live in with his now-fiancée Francesca. She had not quit her job; she continued to fundraise, and CC covered her basic expenses.

The pressure on Daniel began to mount, however, after the Russians displayed their superscientists at the Warsaw press conference. CIA agents questioned Daniel at length and pried into his files and communications to find out if he had leaked any information. He was not beyond suspicion, as they were under tremendous pressure to find someone who had leaked Titan. The head of the CIA had an ominous outlook on the situation: something terribly wrong was going on. The agents understood that Daniel had lost his PP in China, but China was quiet for the moment. Could the Russians have made this great scientific leap on their own? No one in the West believed in the "natural talent" that the Russian government continued to boast about to the world.

Daniel closely watched these events unfold. He asked Dr. Wu to begin human testing of Titan on the disabled first, but government protocol would not allow it. There had to be two years of testing on animals and primates before any Titan chips could be plugged in to the human brain. Daniel continued to plead. He wrote to the president and the head of the CIA and asked for permission to speed up the process. His employers asked him to train his fellow scientists and to hand over more tasks to them, while in theory he was to concentrate on Titan2, which involved high-level usage of Titan and improvements to the original invention.

Daniel quickly began to feel betrayed, as the secretary of defense would meet with Daniel's colleagues behind his back. He would request the meeting minutes from Dr. Wu and ask to be included in future sessions, only to receive ambiguous answers leading him to believe that neither the lab nor the top levels of government trusted him. He knew he could help—he could see that the Russians were already ahead—and the way he was being treated mystified him. If his government would not pay attention to him, then who would? There had to be a place where common sense prevailed, but sadly, he reckoned, that place was not in his own country. As part of Daniel's modified employment agreement, he had agreed that any foreign travel would need to be approved by the head of MHD, and if it were allowed, someone from the Secret Service would travel with him and keep an account of all his activities.

One day Daniel and Francesca were heading up to the High Sierra, near Lake Tahoe, to a place called Camp Sacramento. Daniel had been complaining on the way about the strange work environment and how he does not foresee himself continuing there for much longer. When they reached the little town of Strawberry, California, with a population of 225, Francesca finally built up the courage to admit that she had passed on the Titan patent to Sunny at Gauv Bio. After a brief but wild rage, in which he accused Francesca of betrayal, Daniel calmed down and asked her to take over the wheel.

Still visibly shaken, Daniel wondered, "Did the government suspect this leak? Is that their excuse to have me sidelined? But how could they possibly know?" His mind was spinning. He realized that the snowball had started forming, and there was no way to foresee the results of the leak. He looked up Sunny's coordinates and called him. For Sunny it was late in the evening, exactly twelve hours ahead of PST. Daniel had no breath left to make accusations; he had expended the worst of it on Francesca, and now he just wanted to learn about the progress, if any, on Titan. Sunny could sense the awkwardness of the situation, but he made a quick recovery by assuring Daniel that Guav Bio was desperate for his help and that they had already made humble progress using Titan to treat muscular dystrophy in orphaned children. One of Sunny's remarks especially hit home: "What a shame to have the person responsible for this amazing invention not present to see these kids improving day by day."

Daniel could not completely hide his satisfaction. He replied, "I'm glad you're doing something useful, but I am not completely thrilled with these situations, here and in India. I need to do a lot of thinking."

In reality, Gauv Bio, true to Sunny's promise, had put together a team focused purely on diseases originating in the human brain. Their research had uncovered mutations from the 5hmC that had been layered with healthy DNA on a memristor, which the company had used to combat diseases such as muscular dystrophy and multiple sclerosis. Titan had improved the motor skills of nearly 50 percent of patients and had stopped the progress of these diseases in 90 percent of cases when diagnosed at an early stage.

There was another route of study that Sunny did not know. Dr. Varish Goyal, head of the neurosurgeons at Guav Bio, had been testing his idea of allowing a memristor layered with the same subject's 5hmC DNA to occupy the silicon film without uploading any biodata or corrective mutations. This, he guessed, would essentially give certain areas of the brain room so that the synaptic bulbs (terminals) of dormant neurons could expand. He found his patients at a nursery home, from which he chose the healthiest and the soundest in mind for his experiments. He needed patients who could articulate the difference caused by the treatment, if any were observed.

It turned out that in the human brain, one particular spot mapped by Dr. Goyal — right at the edge of the temporal lobe, known to be responsible for language and speech, and the cerebellum, linked to coordination and movement — encapsulated the brain functions of primitive Paleolithic humans, who shared limited space and lived side by side with mammoths. It was a time when humans could make series of sounds known as crypto-languages. When Titan-style memory was added to this area during experiments, visions that had been passed on by human ancestors came alive, taking advantage of the liberty to expand onto the exterior chip. Patients would describe these visions with similarities that astounded Dr. Goyal's research team. Their euphoria was hard to contain, but a strict secrecy code was enforced, as it was deemed necessary for continuing investigations that were even more potentially groundbreaking. What if history could be rewritten? It was only a matter of time and hard work to find the exact brain regions where recent events lay dormant yet imprinted in the human conscience, ready for the right opportunity to provide a window to the past. Dr. Goyal would term this phenomenon reverse prognostication: visions of the past that humans inherited in addition to the physical and mental attributes of their ancestors.

A young doctor by the name of Chirag suggested that all sorts of crimes, even the old ones, could be solved, and prejudice could be analyzed at its core. In fact, a whole new academic discipline would have to be created, and the definitions and treatments of both psychology and psychiatry would become outdated. Dr. Chirag wrote an impressive essay on this subject, and it would be debated by Indian Prime Minister Kapur, the chief of security, and the head of the health care system, all meeting with the Gauv Bio team, nicknamed the Mojaze ("Miracle") Team.

Daniel finally calmed down, but he hardly spoke. He told Francesca to go back to the Bay Area without him, and he decided to head for India. Francesca asked her last question: "When should I tell the police that you left?"

"Tomorrow," he replied — and that was the last Francesca would hear from him.

Chapter 9

Escape

Daniel packed his clothes and belongings in a backpack. He seemed numb to his surroundings. After trying in vain to stop vehicles on the highway, he walked to Strawberry Village and found a talkative trucker named Vick unloading goods at the general store. The trucker said he was going to the port of Stockton, but he would give Daniel a chance to stop in Sacramento before making the turn. The trucker, a tall and strongly built man with a license to carry arms, did not fear Daniel, who appeared to be a troubled young man headed on an adventure — something the trucker had done before.

Riding in the large semi, Daniel soon stopped answering Vick's questions; he was sound asleep all the way to the I-5 turnoff, when Vick woke him up and told him he was in Sacramento. After giving his thanks, Daniel walked to the harbor district toward the end of Broadway, past the railroad tracks. He could see boats launching from the small pier at the end, and a freight train slowed to make the turn before getting on the steel bridge, heading west. Daniel had seen enough movies to know when and where to jump, and he did it. Barely hanging on to the car, he dangerously stepped to the middle, found a spot on the edge of a milk tanker, and coiled himself up so that he wouldn't be noticed. Daniel thought back to his childhood, when his father took him on the Zephyr train from Oakland with his brother and sister and they met up with his mother in Reno.

At this point he wasn't too concerned with safety. He needed to be off the mainland. He knew the Union Pacific Railroad had a rendezvous with the Bay Railroad Company in San Jose at the southern tip of San Francisco Bay. He made good time, even though his plan to reach India was arduous and complex. He did not want to expose his identity at the airports and figured the best way would be to take a freighter or a private jet. Daniel could afford an exclusive flight, but the risk was too high; he would expose himself to authorities, and although he was not free to leave the country, a record would be kept and the government would know his destination. He had put his trust in Francesca for a second time; he knew that she would not hurt him by telling someone where he was heading. Although Daniel had not told her that he was going to India, she knew that would be the only destination for him. The feeling of being betrayed was beginning to wear off, and he started missing her.

Another train ride took him to San Francisco's Pier 27, where he paid from a secure PayGeo account that he had set up during his stay in Rome. He reached the city by the bay at around 6 p.m., about eleven hours after leaving the campsite in Strawberry. Facing the magnificent Bay Bridge were two cruise ships that unfortunately did not go to Asia, but at 8 p.m. one was headed to Hawaii—2,400 miles in the right direction. The trip would take four days. But how could Daniel board anonymously? He noticed large trucks unloading supplies behind a security gate on the edge of the pier, and forklift operators landing their pallets on the side of the gigantic ship. He decided he needed to look better—his appearance was too shabby—and went to freshen up at the South Beach Café, a place he had frequented during college.

After shaving and cleaning up, Daniel approached the boat's security gate and found the guard on duty eating his sandwich and talking to a truck driver pulling a large trailer. It appeared the two men knew each other well. Daniel snuck behind the trailer, casually walked past the loading area's entrance, and headed toward the busy forklifts that were loading what seemed to be the final lot left on the dock. He had jumped onto the ship and walked toward a second door when an employee yelled at him, "What are you doing here, sir?"

"Well, I made my way down from the top, and for the life of me I can't find my way back up. Can you help me, please?"

"You know, you're the second person today to make it down here. You people can't read English. There are signs everywhere. Follow me."

Daniel kept chatting with the man and said that if he ever made it up to Daniel's level, he would buy him a beer. "Here's the stairs, and there is the elevator," said the worker. "Take care, sir."

Daniel went up the elevator. There was no more risk; obviously he had been cleared to board.

Daniel's backpack was his only nuisance. He found a spot in a hallway at a round, north-facing window and stared at Alcatraz Island at it faded in the distance. He recalled watching the famous movie *Escape from Alcatraz* on one of his family's movie nights.

Daniel blended well in the crowd on the boat, as he met and conversed with tourists. He chose to use the name Alex, as it was his brother's name and he felt comfortable saying it. He spent the time lounging, eating, and sleeping on the corner couches at the salsa bar. Francesca tried to call him several times, but he chose to ignore her. Although he was tempted to answer, he thought it best that she make her story believable by showing failed attempts to reach him.

The following morning, at about 5 a.m., Francesca dialed the emergency channel on RadGio and told the officer who answered at the Twin Bridges station that Daniel was missing. "Yesterday he went on a hike toward Echo Lake and failed to come back," Francesca told the officer. "I was supposed to prepare dinner, but he never showed up. I waited until this morning to report him missing because I was tired—I just went to the tent and slept."

A missing-persons alert was broadcast, and the police began efforts to trace the trail that would have led Daniel to Echo Lake. His physical description reached Livermore Lab and created a panic to find him. Francesca went through grilling interviews; one of the officers suspected foul play and a romance gone wrong. Although she appeared genuine, the security officer at Livermore Lab did not buy her story. She fumbled when she described what sort of meal she was preparing for them both — in fact, she even gave different menu items. Also, she said she had tried to call Daniel only five times — not quite the behavior of a frantic lover.

Nevertheless, a rescue helicopter circled the Echo Lake area night and day in a vain attempt to pick up any signs of Daniel. The temperature had been in the eighties during the day and had dropped to about forty-five degrees at night — mild enough for someone to survive outside. Mountain lions were known to shadow hikers, but there had not been any sightings that season. No one recognized Daniel's photo at the store in Strawberry except the store owner, a man in his late seventies, who thought he had seen Daniel the previous morning but insisted that he could be wrong, as he feared the police would stop looking for Daniel.

Daniel was halfway around the Pacific at a restaurant called Paradiso when one of the tablets on the wall, carrying a San Francisco news channel, showed his picture with the headline "Missing Hiker." He had thus far skillfully managed detection, thanks to the small scissors and shaving kit in his backpack — periodically he would sneak into the men's bathroom, shave yet again, and cut his hair. Daniel did wish to respond to his parents' repeated attempts to reach him, but he was not about to take any risks; the police would inspect their Phonepads, and if he were to answer his plan would be foiled. So far Francesca had played her part well, so there was no need to make matters worse by involving his parents.

The boat docked at Honolulu's Pearl Harbor on the morning of the third day at approximately 10 a.m., and the passengers disembarked. Daniel had second thoughts about continuing his voyage on another luxury liner. Even if there was a boat headed to India's Chennai Port, the time wasted on the water was too valuable. Instead, he wanted to look for a plane headed east. The port was tucked across from a peninsula called Middle Loch near Hickam Air Force Base, while Honolulu's airport stood halfway toward downtown, about seven miles to the south.

Daniel started looking at his many flight options and found a nonstop flight departing at 8 p.m. and landing him in Bangalore in five hours. He could not book any seats because he needed travel documents that did not have his name on them. Although electronic passports were permissible, he could not use his as it was automatically recorded and traceable by U.S agencies. He took a cab downtown toward the address of a private jet company called Blue Star, whose office was near the airport. Daniel was taking a gamble by relying on his charm — coupled with money from his secret Italian PayGeo account — to find a jet and a pilot that will take him to Bangalore. He had looked up Alexander Vale before deciding to use this name, all the while remembering that his brother Alexander was buying a home in Sunnyvale, a combination that was not easy to forget or to stumble upon.

In the meantime a full alert went to all U.S. ports of entry to be on the lookout for anyone matching Daniel Oakley's name and description; he was to be handed to the authorities immediately. Daniel had decided that he would walk into Blue Star's office as a spoiled, wealthy individual demanding to see the interiors of the planes before booking any flights. The reception was extremely cordial; Daniel had managed to shower and clean up on the boat, and he looked good for the part he was playing. Although the sales associate, a young lady by the name of Maya, thought he was spoiled, she found him charming as well. She and Daniel sat in a mock-up of an airplane room and discussed the various sales programs—fixed-rate yearly flights, twenty or thirty hours prorated, and so on. Meanwhile, the curved screens on the walls showed the different interiors of planes in their inventory.

At one point Daniel asked Maya to pause. "That's what I like," he said.

"Great. It's our best model: the Gulfstream 2018A, with a twin engine—"

"That's fine. I'll book one now to Bangalore if you can arrange it."

Maya was ecstatic. Clients rarely came in without an appointments, and when they did, they were mostly old and miserable, and they made a ruckus before they settled on what they wanted. Daniel offered to sign a yearlong contract and to pay the entire amount immediately.

First, Maya had some details to tend to. She asked Daniel to transfer a handshake ID from his Phonepad to hers. Daniel shook his head and said, "Well, Maya, that's the only problem. I can't do that. I am Alexander Vale—you can look me up—and I am not a criminal. I am a stockbroker, and I'm willing to give you a handsome gift."

Daniel was in luck. Maya asked if he was doing anything illegal—a drug run, an escape from jail, or the like. He asked her to look up his name and find out for herself. He just wanted to leave the country anonymously, that was all, and he would pay what it took to do it.

Maya was more than willing to accommodate his request. The challenge, however, would be the exit and entry at the official gates at both borders. She said she needed someone's ID, which was hard for anyone to give up. Everything had to match—his fingerprints, his face, the veins in his hands, his irises. . . . "And you can't steal one," Maya said. "You can't download an epassport document without the person's consent, because it's encrypted."

Throughout the conversation Daniel was as charming, eloquent, and convincing as possible. He repeatedly told Maya how nice it would be to get away without being tracked and asked her simply to be creative. "What would it take, Maya, really?"

Maya asked Daniel to return the following day. In the meantime she would investigate ways to fulfill his request. She knew that Daniel (Alex) was taking a risk as well — she could easily alert authorities to his plan, but she didn't. She saw that he had goodness in him and was definitely not a criminal. Nevertheless, Maya would look at the FBI's and CIA's most-wanted lists after work to satisfy herself that she was not helping an outlaw escape justice.

Later that night Maya tried convincing her fiancé Andrew to let Daniel use his ID, thus gaining free travel for two people for the entire year, in addition to the gift that Alex had promised her. Andrew refused her proposal but suggested that his disabled cousin would probably fit the bill. His cousin was in a miserable state after falling during a hike on the Na Pali cliffs in Kauai. There were security issues, such as an iris check and a vein imprint, that Maya had to circumvent, but Andrew could update his cousin's profile and replace it with Alex's. Daniel's new name would be Adam Akamu.

Maya was risking a lot, but she had seen her boss making odd arrangements with Brazilian customers who had most likely been dealing drugs. In this case, Alex looked clean on record — even if he was not using his real name. That night Maya spent more time trying unsuccessfully to recognize Daniel's face among wanted fugitives posted worldwide. And as it turned out, she was certainly out of luck when it came to finding his face on any list of criminals. Daniel was only banned from travel, and the order was part of an internal communiqué that was not published in the public domain. Maya was looking in the wrong places.

The next morning, Andrew took Daniel to visit Adam at the hospital. The plan seemed straightforward. Andrew would ask Adam's mother for his Phonepad, and then he would reenter Alex's facial-recognition features, vein scan, iris scan, and fingerprint. Thus, Alex would assume Andrew's complete identity for the flight. There was a brief setback when Adam's mom did not know his short password to begin, but that was cleared up when Adam, lying in bed in a vegetative state, was able to satisfy the Phonepad's protocol to make all the necessary changes.

Daniel (Alex) was now a permanently disabled man from the state of Hawaii. He would reach Bangalore the next day, after transferring the equivalent of Blue Star's annual subscription fee to Maya's PayGeo account. Feeling very lucky, he promised Maya that he would try to help Adam one day.

Cruise Ship loading area

Chapter 10

Dr. Adam Akamu

Daniel called Sunny as soon as he cleared customs in Bangalore. He was taken immediately to the countryside, where he would be Sunny's guest for the duration of his stay. The two men got along well; Daniel had forgiven the past and was concerned only with the future. Sunny and Daniel agreed that the Russians and Chinese had likely gotten hold of his patent. After Daniel had lost his Phonepad in Shenzhen, either the kill command had not worked or the thieves' technical abilities had enabled them to copy the files before they could be destroyed. It had been a planned robbery, and the conniving Dr. Su had revealed Daniel's moves to the MSS; that was Daniel's theory, and he stuck to it.

Sunny had been working for India's secret service, the Research and Analysis Wing (RAW), all along and had made a good name for himself, as he had been credited for passing Daniel's patent to Gauv Bio. Daniel was not only welcomed, but also offered a drug similar to the famous X treatment done in China — however, Guav claimed that this drug was a completely Indian discovery that worked more quickly than the Chinese version. Daniel did not think that taking this drug treatment was necessary; he did not mind the simpler procedure, which meant matching his fingerprints to those of Adam Akamu, he was not going to take a chance being discovered in the event he had to leave India. Sunny continued to run down the list of the many ways he can be in disguise in case the need arises, which included facial-recognition alteration techniques and even the most complex forms of vein recognition. Sunny revealed to Daniel a new procedure of duplicating an invisible glove that mimicked the veins of anyone on record. Although impressed, Daniel politely asked for permission to work only at Gauv Bio, particularly in the company's zero-gravity lab, while he lay low for the time being.

Back in the United States, Daniel's parents were at a loss. They were afraid he had been eaten by wolves or lions, or had fallen into a crevice. Robert had lost weight, and a major depression had set in. Ama simply would not believe that her son was dead. All the while, the CIA had been monitoring the Oakley family through listening devices planted in and around the house and their vehicles. It had become difficult to intercept incoming calls on the Oakley's' Phonepads; the security was too high, and it required too much work to tap these sophisticated machines. The old-fashioned listening devices sufficed to prove that Daniel had not made contact with his parents, thus leading the CIA to believe that Francesca had had a hand in Daniel's disappearance—and possibly his death.

The FBI rigorously questioned Francesca about the discrepancies within her cooking stories, Daniel's sudden plan to go on a hike, and her act of calling Daniel only five times when she was worried and did not know his whereabouts. She had flunked the lie-detector test the first time, and investigators had continued to press her to retell her story numerous times. Finally they suggested that she get an attorney because they intended to levy criminal charges— including murder. Soon after that, Francesca broke down and told the authorities what she knew, which was not quite the entire story. The thought of going to jail in America was more than Francesca could bear. She had lived her life in luxury and among global diplomatic circles. Besides, it was already two weeks after Daniel's "disappearance," and he had likely reached India already.

Francesca decided not to divulge where Daniel had gone. In the fifth hour of interrogation at the FBI office in San Francisco, she buckled. "Daniel packed his bag and left. I don't know where he went, but he told me to say that he was gone by the time I woke up. That is all I know."

The agents were relieved that Daniel was not dead. They had vindicated their suspicion about the entire story, but they decided not to let his parents know that they believed he was still alive. Further questioning of Francesca yielded no results; she stuck to her answers, and her second lie-detector test was inconclusive. The results were passed on to the U.S. Department of Homeland Security, which was responsible for delaying the publishing of Daniel's name and photos four days after his disappearance. Had they sent his profile to the various media channels and the infinite live broadcasts on RadGio right away, they would have stood a chance of catching him, but the time wasted presuming he was lost in the High Sierra had allowed Daniel to slip away.

The CIA had been trying hard to understand the situations in China and Russia. Its agents had been given a faint picture of these scientific events, but without knowing more specifics about Titan, it was hard to put all the pieces together. At the White House, at a meeting including the secretary of defense, the head of the FDA, and the secretary of state, the head of the CIA summed it up in a tumultuous exchange with the president. "Although the physical apprehension of Daniel would indeed be welcomed, the problem is far bigger," he said. "In the past few months China and Russia have gained a noticeable advantage that would require a lot of catching up. I cannot believe what I am about to suggest, Mr. President. This is the first time that we ought to relax our laws on testing and take a proactive role. We should create our own heroes and apostles and whatever the hell they're calling them. This is an American invention by our own scientist, and we are losing our grip on it, first by toying with a kid and giving him a stack of conditions up the yinyang and causing him to run away. It's absurd, Mr. President, how far we have gone. We've completely dropped the ball. I'm for getting this Dr. Wu in front of us and getting his goddamned lab to start showing us some beef, Mr. President. Excuse my language, but I am sick and tired of having wasted, oh, a year or so, when this kid was right here with us, in this room, and what have we got to show for it? Zilch."

The president answered, "Daniel wrote to us here at the White House and asked us to get off our high horses and get to work. The kid knew what was going on, but we didn't. Now I understand this predicament we are in. I cannot and will not allow any nation on Earth to hold us hostage, be it with their technology, our technology, or their superweapons. I will not allow it, period. Matt is suggesting that we relax our laws governing testing. That's what Oakley has been saying all along. And hell, it wouldn't be the first time. You all read about World War II and how the A-bomb was handled, the secret missions and the advantages we gave to scientists to come from Germany and Russia. Well, we ought to take some liberties ourselves. What do you say, Phil?"

Secretary Sheridan responded, "Although this country was built on individual achievements and taking risks and so on, sir, I do not want us to blame ourselves anymore. We did what the book says (in reference to the Guidelines), and we've done it before. Let's put together a plan right here, get Dr. Wu on a conference call and ask about their progress in the lab and find out what's going on. Maybe they are already working on our American superman. I pray they are."

Years later, the president would write in his biography about this meeting:

> I felt that I had betrayed my country, my oath, knowing the Russians and the Chinese had already produced extraordinary results on their damn test-tube scientists, using our own technologies. It reminded me of the wartimes and difficulties that our nation and its presidents had endured. Although the future looked bleak, I had no choice but to order a scientific mobilization on all fronts, private and military, on the largest possible scale. I told my cabinet that we had to build our new liberty ships and produce soldiers, scientists, astronauts, brainy good old Americans of the likes that no one would dare threaten our interest. We would not be caught unprepared; it was our mission yet again to rescue freedom and the human race, just as

our great-grandfathers had fought the Nazis of Europe. I impressed on the House Committee on Intelligence how serious and dangerous the situation was and begged them to do their level best. One member commented on how I was speaking in war terms, such as when I reminded them of Churchill's World War II defiance against Hitler: "We will never surrender. . . . if we were to lose let it be our finest hour." I also brought up the Japanese general's comment about awakening the giant and told everyone, "We need to show the free people in the world that we are still giants and have a fighting spirit."

The president understood the gravity of the situation. This time the enemy could win the war without firing a single bullet. Everything they knew was at stake: satellites, cybersecurity, the entire nation's defenses. . . . If they chose, the enemy could intercept and decode every vital command residing anywhere, safety would be provisional, and they may stop every call, hamper transportation, and turn off power grids to the entire nation, including the lights at the White House. Mathew Cavers's concerns were real and warranted. The nation had to act.

True to his promise, the president swiftly put into motion a bill that was approved unanimously by both houses of Congress. Under the new law, the nation would invest in Titan research and produce the first American superhumans, which would become known as Titans. Although the details of the project were kept secret in theory, the administration purposely leaked the general concept, partly to ease the American public's increasing anxiety but mainly to tell the world that the "giant" would be awakened yet again. The first breed of superhuman to see the light in public would be at Stanford less than a year after the announcement of the new law, a fitting place for Titan's birth, beating Livermore Lab at producing their first superhuman by just two days.

By this time the Titan frenzy had intensified, and the Russians and Chinese were parading their hybrid humans, who dazzled the world with their extraordinary abilities. The United States called for a UN Security Council meeting that both

Russia and China refused to attend. Russia's premier, after attending a meeting with his Chinese counterpart, would remark to reporters, "We are tired of American movies, no? That's why we don't think the UN meeting is necessary." Meanwhile, the Chinese premier, Mr. Wei, said, "The Chinese mind was not born yesterday. I think Americans have to study our history more." Then, smiling, both leaders turned their backs and walked away from their audiences.

In a desperate attempt to save face, the U.S. government sued China and Russia at the World Court. The Americans accused both countries of technology theft and infringement on the Titan patent. Although it was in essence a valid argument, it was meant more for propaganda purposes. The international judges later gave an inconclusive ruling on the matter, but even if the verdict had been in the Americans' favor, nothing could have been done; everyone in government would have known that it was a waste of time and no one would be able to reverse the events.

A G22 summit called by India at the behest of its American friends, desperate to bring their rivals to the table, failed to produce any results. Although the official purpose for the meeting had SAE title (Stop Altering Evolution) the official press release had a headline 'Stopping Proliferation and the Alteration of Human Evolution', China and Russia refused even to acknowledge the existence of such programs or of artificial "smart chip" implants. Meanwhile, India's leaders played their cards well. They lacked China and Russia's inherit dislike for the United States, and their brand of competitiveness had thus far been limited to benign research. India admitted that its scientists were working on similar chips designed to combat diseases, and a federal licensing agreement was drawn in exchange for royalties paid to the U.S. government. This was a most lenient agreement for both sides, which were desperate to achieve the appearance of a balance of power between Russia and China on the one hand, and the U.S and India on the other. Europe had followed the lead of the United States in condemning these 'Evolution Altering programs' as they were referred to on the European continent.

Ralph Hänsel, head of the European Parliament, went as far as saying that "nobody can outfox human beings. Our friends in the East, Russia and China, should know that they may win the small wars of today, but they will lose the war against us. God forbid if it happened. Why do I say that? Because we see arrogance, and we have seen arrogance before, especially in Europe, where we paid dearly in millions of lives. Stop parading your scientists and athletes. It is an insult to your fellow man, because you know and we know that this new technology came from this side. Let's use it to make friends, not enemies. I tell you, our friends, come to the table, put your grievances there if you have any, and stop playing cat and mouse with us. It's a crime to your people to be led to a state of superiority over your brothers and sisters; it will destroy everyone. Please, our dear friends of the East, we know you had and still have a humble culture, and you revere God and fellow humans. Come and talk to us. We are one and the same as you." It was a very telling speech from a known liberal, who had not been shy about speaking of his contempt of the United States and its technical domination just a year ago.

Daniel had lived in India for over eight months, and he had closely followed events as they had unfolded. He could not believe that the world had changed so much in this relatively short period of time, His name was synonymous with *traitor* in the United States, and he was glad that he was presumed dead. He was becoming a loner, but he refused to give up and remain a spectator. Instead, he was thinking of ways to make a change and possibly resurface. At Gauv Bio, he headed a team responsible for research on cognitive diseases. He had an elaborate facility with a zero-gravity lab dedicated to his team. They all knew who he was, but they were discreet, as RAW had informed them that divulging his secret could jeopardize Indian national security and put his life and those of the rest of their team members at risk—essentially, RAW scared them into believing that Daniel was wanted dead or alive.

Daniel, now Dr. Adam, made important breakthroughs in areas such as multiple sclerosis and Canavan disease. He enjoyed his work, as he was in the company of excellent researchers. The Indian government pretended they did not know who he was. On the surface, Daniel Oakley did not exist in India, he had broken no laws, and no warrant for his arrest was issued, at least not under his current name Adam Akamu. India did not disclose his presence at the G22 summit when asked by the U.S. secretary of state. They were glad to have Dr. Adam listed as one of their own on the dynamic worldwide list of discoveries in the biophysics field. The Indian government even offered Dr. Adam citizenship in honor of his work.

Daniel began to see how the world had changed in the two years since he had succeeded at improving the physical and mental performance of rats and mice. It was now an abnormal world in which humans artificially improved other humans who had no illness, except for their own or their government's quest for power. As nations settled old grievances, they created a class of political egocentrics with Titan implants. This group eventually became known as the Poliegotitians (politician with inflated egos) in historical records. They desired supreme knowledge that would allow them to outmaneuver, outsmart, and outperform their counterparts in a race for technical and economical supremacy—and, sadly, military dominance—on the world stage.

Daniel accepted that he was no longer relevant; he had been forgotten as serious events had taken shape. He was at a great disadvantage, as he no longer held any control; when mentioned in the United States, his name barely elicited a reaction, as he was still presumed dead or lost somewhere in California. His name in India was now Dr. Adam Akamu. Although he felt his new name was a coincidence; it was ironic that he was the new Adam, the father who had sinned and brought to light this new human breed that would cause a second human damnation. "How is it," he pondered, "that we have come this far, and how will it all end?"

Daniel began to notice how he resembled his father — the way he moved, how he walked, and even his taste for music. He remembered being a little boy and driving around in his dad's old convertible as they blasted symphonies from dead composers of past centuries, like Bach, Mendelssohn, and Beethoven, now playing on his RadGio. He was feeling homesick and debating whether he should call his parents. He correctly assumed that they were under surveillance, but recently the FBI had quit monitoring the Oakleys altogether, as Homeland Security had dropped Daniel's arrest warrant.

It was unclear why the warrant had been dropped; the assumption was that the department had far more important work and limited resources. The other possible explanation was that Daniel had not broken the law entirely; he had breached his contract with the government by leaving his job and the country, but apparently it was not a clear enough violation to warrant an arrest. The biggest surprise to Daniel was that the government continued paying his full salary, which was deposited in his local (and inactive) PayGeo account, which remained under watch.

At night, under the big skies of Hosur, a small town south of Bangalore, Daniel sat on his balcony in his luxurious apartment and let his mind wander. His soul searching led him to tally the people he had disappointed in his life. The list was immense, especially when he included people that he despised. Then he narrowed it down to the people he cared for the most but still had disappointed; his parents, his brother and sister, Francesca, his friends and colleagues at Stanford, Anaya, Mirvet, the little kids he saw in Egypt, and Adam, the poor soul in the Honolulu hospital who made it possible for him to leave the country undetected. Although he was a loner in general, he would meet up with Sunny off and on. He failed to get close to anyone of the opposite sex; he did not feel ready for a new romance, as he still hoped that one day he would reunite with Francesca.

Chapter 11

The Nirvana Triangle

Recently Daniel had become closer to Dr. Goyal, who secretly briefed him on the amazing new research on implants in the primitive part of the brain, the cerebellum and temporal lobe areas. Humankind's entire history was about to be rewritten. Daniel and Dr. Goyal began to meet often after work and try to make sense of the new science that was gripping the world's superpowers. They grappled with the psychological ramifications as well as the big philosophical question: was the Titan stage of evolution inevitable, or were human beings really even capable of reaching such a stage? In their conversations they would question the meaning and existence of life itself.

Dr. Goyal clung to his Hindu beliefs. He enthusiastically explained henotheism, or the devotion to a single god while accepting the existence of others. He wanted Daniel to understand the journey to *mokṣa* (the release) as the final purpose of life taught by Brahma, and he felt that this journey could be confirmed through the Titan implants. Dr. Goyal shared fantastic data about patients, who revealed the reincarnated lives of their ancestors and, through their ancient observing eyes, confirmed the belief in samsara, which meant that an earthly life was one of suffering and subject to repeated deaths and births. Titan, Dr. Goyal concluded, would indeed allow humankind to achieve mokṣa.

Daniel asked Dr. Goyal if he could attend a questioning session with him and his patients. It did not take long. Dr. Goyal called Daniel one evening and asked him to come back to the lab at Gauv Bio to confirm the findings for himself.

As Dr. Goyal examined two patients in their seventies, Daniel sat and watched while using his Phonepad for immediate translations of their answers. He was shocked to hear the patients, who had received their implants less than a month earlier, talking about their past lives. They said they had died 148 years back, and they recited their old names and ranks in the British East Indian Company. The two patients recognized each other and became emotional as they talked about the people they knew, the places they had gone, and the British officers who had trained them. It was like an episode from a movie, except no one knew how to act because the screenplay was so extensive.

Daniel was suddenly reminded about the dreams he had been having about his father, and he wondered what it all meant. Before his eyes, he was being transported into a realm that he wanted to experience. He did not care about increasing his intellectual capabilities like the "heroes" or the "apostles"; he wanted to know more about his own past.

Daniel knew all about the well-studied zones in the human brain. He knew that memory "resided" in the cortex and the hippocampus, but he also understood that memory was one of the hardest phenomena to pin down. Scientist had struggled to categorize the many types, including remote memory, declarative memory, episodic memory, and semantic memory, among many others. Apparently Dr. Goyal knew exactly where to look for memory it; he manipulated his nanowire with extreme precision and unleashed the dormant neurons that were loaded with information yet static, revealing the magnitude of embedded information. Daniel was impressed with how Dr. Goyal managed to connect three implants working in tandem to elicit inherited, ancient memories. Dr. Goyal called these implants the nirvana triangle: one in the hippocampus, one in the frontal cortex, and one in the left side of the temporal lobe.

Dr. Goyal hoped his remarkable discovery would balance the technical mischief of this new human, keeping humankind tied to its natural roots by remembering its ancestral path and its struggle for continuity through many generations. He would soon argue that the nirvana triangle was the only answer to what was shaping up to be a methodical game of chess that had no winners in the end: the quest for world dominance. That quest, he predicted, was bound to lead humanity to its ultimate annihilation if the nirvana triangle were not employed.

Dr. Goyal felt it was critical to convince scientists to believe in his theories, especially the scientists with authority. He contended that there was practically no data on this particular type of Titan, so it would be cheaper to mass-produce and to sell, and the procedure could take one hour instead of the three that it currently took. This was a romantic argument whose outcome no one could predict. The chip was actually far from being economically practical to produce; neither was it humanly possible to train doctors in so many nations on the complex implantation procedure—assuming those nations even agreed to implement it. Even if there were a theoretical conveyor belt to handle the billions of humans worldwide, spending one hour to implant the chips in each one would take thousands of years.

But Daniel remained intrigued, and he asked to have the nirvana triangle installed in his own brain. Dr. Goyal had by now completed about twenty-five such procedures, so he had no problem putting Daniel to sleep and installing the three memristors with laser precision.

What happened to Daniel next took him on a new life quest that would explain his ancestral past and his adventurous nature, leading him toward an unusual journey, both physical and emotional.

Daniel's first night of sleep with the chips was uneventful; he woke up feeling a slight sore and an itch at the spots where Titans had been implanted. However, the next night, as he slept, he began seeing odd visions. First he was on a dock where everyone was dressed in thick, dark clothes, with women carrying funny umbrellas. In his sleep, he noted that the scene resembled a painting by Monet.

Then he found himself walking toward a large ship with a young man who spoke a weird language.

The next night he managed to enter the same scene, but this time he was carrying a document that looked like a passport, but with an Ottoman Turk insignia. Oddly, the name on the document was Yosef Ballout. His friend, the young man, was calling to him and again talking in a language that was very familiar but incomprehensible. The friend gave Daniel a second set of passport-like documents in the name of Amin Ballout. "Was that my brother?" he wondered. "No, he was a cousin; I'm sure of it." Finally he and his friend reached a little booth with two police officers wearing funny old round hats that looked like kettles and had odd metal stamps on the front.

Then both people appeared in his vision, they were splitting up: Amin went on the larger boat, while Yosef walked toward another. Yosef continued boarding, having left his large black leather bag at the pier with the number 4464 written on it. He had the second part of that ticket in his chest pocket, and he kept on feeling it now and then to make sure it was still there.

Daniel began recording these events on his PP, but he realized there was no need to do it—these events were glued in his memory. He could not possibly forget them, because his memory had so much extra space!

Scenes would come and go. Once he was in a clothing store, and this time people were speaking in Spanish. He had a vision of riots on the streets, and newspapers with headline reading "Disturbios de la ciudad". This was in Mexico, which was a reasonable place since his grandfather and great-grandfather had been there. He knew that he had Mediterranean origins on his father's side; they were from Lebanon, a tiny country in the Levant that had struggled throughout its existence. But what about the name Ballout? Soon he was able to explain it with certainty: apparently his grandfather had switched Ballout with Oak, and then Oakley, a translation of the Arabic word for "oak tree" or "acorn."

Arabic

السِــــــنديان ,بلــــوط

البلـــــوط شـجر

Pronounced: ba-LOOT or ba-LOUT

Similar Words	Part of Speech
oak	N

Dictionaire Internationale

During his visions he also visited Topeka, Kansas, where he found his cousin, who was called Herman instead of Ameen. Herman was in an altercation with two thieves behind the counter of a hardware store, and he shot one of them. He saw blood on his face and called out, "Bev! Bev!?"

As the days went on, Daniel began undergoing a subtle identity crisis. He knew the reason for it but was still uncomfortable; he wanted to know more about his past. The implants were working very well; he was able to recall the circulating scenes in his mind on demand and pick up where he had left off. Daniel wondered if schizophrenics were that way, having been cursed with a nirvana triangle instead of being blessed with it. Doomed to mental illness, they existed in a realm that they could not escape as freely as Daniel could.

Chapter 12

Keeping a Promise

Daniel had some unfinished business. Now that he was an Indian citizen, he was free to move. He felt a desperate need to fulfill his obligations to the folks he had promised to help, and he decided to start in Cairo. He would see Mirvet and bring the little girl Sara and her father Adel to India for treatment. He asked Dr. Goyal to use his influence to find a room for a new patient and to be prepared if Daniel were able to bring her back. Everyone at Guav Bio liked and respected Daniel, and they were willing to accommodate him. RAW gave him permission to travel after he signed a pledge of secrecy as to divulge the Guav Bio projects and promised to return within three weeks — with a clause for indefinite renewal. Daniel wished that his native country had shown him the same trust.

It had been a year since Daniel had spoken to Mirvet. When they spoke over RadGio, she was surprised that he introduced himself as Adam and kept his camera turned off.

Mirvet knew exactly who he was. "You are Daniel!" she said with great excitement.

"I call myself Adam now. Please be discreet."

Due to the fact that 80 percent of PPs were equipped with a voice-recognition feature, Mirvet was probably going to find out Daniel's identity anyway. He told her that he would be flying to Cairo to visit her friend Sara and wondered if they could travel to India, preferably with both parents, for her treatment. After a brief pause, she answered, "No problem. We'll get the passports ready in a few days."

Dr. Adam Akamu landed in Cairo undisturbed, and Mirvet and Adel met him outside the airport. Mirvet, looking extremely pretty in an orange dress dotted with tiny yellow and brown flowers, gave him a big hug. Adel, standing by the car, gave Dr. Akamu a hug as well. Daniel sat in front. This time he felt better about Egypt's driving conditions; after witnessing so many horrific maneuvers by the drivers in India, Cairo felt tame. Adel was driving an electric hydrogen car made by Peugeot Egypt, a plant built by the French to supply the local markets. But Adel was really more of country man, unshaven and wearing the traditional long garb of a farmer. Mirvet, on the other hand, could pass for a French model due to her striking beauty, though she had a more voluptuous body. The pair was a strange contradiction.

Daniel asked if he could see Sara that same day, but Mirvet declared that they had other plans for him. They drove to their village, Izbat Al Ghaffar, which was right outside Cairo, where Sara's entire family was waiting for with a lamb feast in Daniel's honor. The dish, called *mansaf*, was made of lamb chops cooked in a sauce of fermented dried yogurt and served with rice or bulgur. They called it Dorra's dish, after a Jordanian cook who seemed to run the house.

Daniel was very appreciative and moved by the gesture, and he felt additional pressure not to disappoint them. He hoped that his friends at Gauv Bio could help Sara, who was not yet officially diagnosed. Mirvet said that Sara most likely had SMA, or spinal muscular atrophy. Her doctors in Cairo described it as type 3, which was the least severe (types 1 and 2 were usually deadly), but it would still confine her to a wheelchair.

The family gave Daniel a warm reception, and although he was not supposed to understand what they were saying, he found himself picking up on words that seemed familiar to him. It seemed like a new facet of the nirvana triangle: if his ancestors spoke Arabic in the Levant, or Greek before that, was it possible that he could understand languages that rode along with visions from the past? The Egyptian dialect was different from the Lebanese one, but there were a lot of similarities.

Adel resisted sending Daniel to his hotel and offered his humble house instead. Eventually, however, he was satisfied that everything was prepaid and it would be a waste of money for Daniel not to stay at the hotel. Besides, Daniel had assured him that he would be back the next day to talk about the next steps.

The "docteur," as Adel referred to Daniel, met with the family the next day at Dorra's house and agreed to leave as soon as he could arrange for flights. The passports arrived that same day, as planned. Egyptian passports were issued on paper or in electronic form, loaded onto PPs. The family had chosen paper for the simple reason that Sara could neither move nor speak, and these were essential abilities for using epassports. Daniel was curious to see these crisp passports, as he's never seen one before. Adel handed him the stack. They were written in both Arabic and English, and, to his amazement, Sara's mother was listed as Mirvet!

Daniel was visibly shaken, and Adel asked Mirvet to explain. Sara was actually Mirvet's niece. Sara's real mother had died at birth, and Mirvet had agreed to adopt her as a token of affection to her older sister, who had raised Mirvet after they lost their own mother at a very young age. Mirvet had been able to take complete, official custody of Sara, but she needed to work to support her family.

Later, Mirvet would tell Daniel that Adel had remarried and had no children with his new wife, Dorra, the supposed cook. Adel had met Dorra in an unusual way. During a trip to Jordan, while delivering goods to Amman, Adel saw a woman being chased by her violent husband. He offered her a hiding place in the back of his truck and promised to marry her as soon as they set foot in Egypt. Dorra was unable to have children, and her husband had become very cruel, especially that particular evening. Kids on the street had called him *akhim* ("infertile"), which had triggered a violent outburst causing his wife to run for her life. Infertility remained a shameful problem in that part of the world. It was a sad story, but Adel kept his smile nevertheless.

Daniel turned to Mirvet and saw tears in her eyes. "I hope nothing goes wrong in India," he thought.

After arriving in India, the group stayed at Daniel's spacious apartment, a considerable upgrade from their humble home in Ghagar village. It did not take long for the Indian scientists to discover the 5hmC SMN mutation needed to put in a silicon memristor to treat Sara. Her disease, SMA, involved a genetic mutation that caused to body to produce a protein called SMN. This protein disrupted the blood supply to the muscles and led to further damage. They knew that existing drugs called HDAC inhibitors became ineffective in SMA patients after a short period and could actually do more harm. But when the brain took over with calibrated self regulating commands to produce SMN, replicating it from an exact mutation sample from the patient, a continuous regulated supply on a as needed basis would be injected to the patient's blood stream.

The time Daniel spent with Mirvet while Sara was at Guav Bio was pivotal. Adel returned to Egypt after two weeks, as he felt useless and unable to function freely in a place that he did not understand. Daniel was very physically attracted to Mirvet, who consistently wore very revealing dresses in the sweltering heat for which Bangalore was famous for. He knew he loved Francesca, but he had not spoken to her since he had left that camp in California, and he would probably never see her again. Mirvet was in India, staying in his apartment, and alone. Besides, she was more than willing to be intimate with him. He was unsure about how it would play out in the future—he had not been very impressed with Mirvet's intellect and opinions—but she was too sweet to ignore. They embarked on an unusual relationship, filled with both guilt and love.

After becoming more comfortable with the relationship, Mirvet began calling Daniel "love." She wanted to share a deeper secret, and asked Daniel for forgiveness before telling him. Daniel refused, joking that since the age of six, he had never given an opinion about something he didn't know. Mirvet looked serious, but Daniel wouldn't budge, even though he had become very curious.

"What is it? Are you married?" Daniel asked.

"No, silly guy."

"Do you have kids?"

"No."

"Go ahead, tell me."

"You still might get mad—no, actually, you *will* get mad. Please promise me not to."

"I will not, and don't tell me." It was a simple trick Daniel had mastered from childhood. Although he was impatient on many levels, he knew patience worked best in these circumstances.

Mirvet, on the other hand, had zero patience, and after about five minutes of pure silence she decided to speak. She admitted that she was the one who had stabbed him on the boat mistaken him for the cook over two years ago. For his part, Daniel admitted that he had been following her. Mirvet further revealed that she had made a deal with Hedeco, the Japanese woman on board, who had recruited her help earlier to poison the cook. Apparently the cook had molested Hedeco when she was just thirteen on a trip with her parents almost twenty years earlier. Remembering his name and occupation, she had planned her revenge. Hedeco had asked Mirvet to make sure they booked their Nile trip with the cook onboard. Then she had hatched a plan to poison him by dropping a highly concentrated and soluble cyanide pill in his water before he went to bed, as he was known to carry a water bottle all the time. Hedeco had promised to pay Mirvet a half million G to administer the pill. The money was to go straight into Adel's account to help take care of Sara. Mirvet lost the pill that evening, however, when the pressure from Hedeco to do the deed made her extremely agitated and when she told Hedeco that she did not have the pill anymore, Hedeco increased the reward to one million G — provided Mirvet could find a way to get rid of the cook.

Daniel was stunned by this incredible account. "Why didn't Hedeco go to the police when she was thirteen? That's an age when you understand a lot. Or she could have gone to the police at age twenty, or thirty. Why did she take matters into her own hands? What a way to ruin more lives." He was shocked at what money could buy and disappointed that Mirvet would agree to do such a thing — and he was vocal about his displeasure with her. "So, Mirvet, what if I had died on that boat? How would you feel?"

"Terrible," she replied.

"Well, that's not enough. I feel 'terrible' when I stain the carpet! I am shocked that you could carry out such an offense. What if you had been caught?"

"Well, I wasn't caught, and you survived," Mirvet pointed out. "We are here, and I am in love with you, and that's what matters. Please don't lecture me. I told you about this because I love you, and you want me to tell you everything from now on, right? Besides, Hedeco planned it, and it was her fault too, you know. And one more thing: that cook was a lowlife who deserved to die."

"Mirvet, this is serious stuff. Why didn't Hedeco do the whole thing? I know why. She found someone like you to do the dirty work — that's the way I see it. And you talk about that cook as if you would do it all over again. Did you get any money?"

"Only the half million."

"She shorted you, that crook! Do you think you deserved the million?" Daniel taunted sarcastically.

"Look, Daniel, don't hurt me, please. I'm not happy about this, okay?"

"Great. Maybe you should ask Hedeco for the balance, or you'll kill her."

"Enough, Daniel. I think you've made up your mind about me now, haven't you?"

"Mirvet, dear, I can't walk around ignoring this with hugs and kisses. I can't. Yes, it says a lot about you, and frankly I need to think this whole thing over. For me it's not business as usual."

Sara was miraculously improving. She was able to move her legs with ease for the first time. Her hands had remained fairly healthy, but now she had better dexterity. The clinic staff was ecstatic to see her smile, and on the fourth week, she was able to take her first steps. Daniel was assured that she would make a quick recovery.

Daniel's relationship with Mirvet had grown cold. He began to see an immature side to her. She was not a deep thinker, and their philosophical conversations were usually one-dimensional. Francesca had been able to debate with him on a higher level, and she would make him change his mind about strongly held opinions that he thought were sacred. Mirvet would never compare. Sadly, he realized that people were not all created equal. Not everyone could be a soccer player, an artist, or a philosopher. It wasn't always due to environment; it was just life. He made up his mind to break up with her, and once Sara checked out of the lab, he said his final good-bye to both of them as they went back to Egypt.

Daniel appreciated Mirvet's honesty, but at the same time he was very disappointed.

Chapter 12

The Triangle Completed

Daniel's next move was toward his parents and Francesca. He had hesitated about calling them for months, but now the time had come, and what better way to reconnect than to pay a surprise visit? He was an Indian national, so he needed an entry visa for the United States. He picked a time when some of his colleagues were scheduled to speak at a highly publicized conference, SAE 2 (Stop Altering Evolution). A low-level Chinese delegation had promised to attend, while the Russians had refused. Gauv Bio bundled their visa requests electronically and sent their epassports to the embassy at Bangalore. The approval came in, and Dr. Adam Akamu was granted a visitor's visa to the USA.

Daniel purchased a private eticket that had a layover in San Francisco before ostensibly going to Chicago well before the conference. His visions of the past had accumulated, and he needed someone to help him make sense of it all. Lately his visions were taking place in La Paz, Bolivia, where he was dying and had a high fever in a cabin. This vision had to be recent—at least after the New World had been discovered.

The plane landed at about 4 p.m. Daniel passed the immigration checkpoint, where his iris scan was logged and his vein prints were checked against his epassport. Part of the immigration officer's job description was to engage newcomers in conversation, *any* conversation, so Daniel had to speak English with a fake Indian accent. The officer, a gentle Asian American, complimented Daniel: "You speak pretty good English, you know."

Daniel replied, "Dank you."

The cab ride was short. Daniel asked the driver to drop him off a few hundred feet away from his parents' house. He was looking for shock value. Besides, the different location might come in handy one day if taxi drivers were to show their logs somewhere, somehow.

He could tell immediately that his dad was not home, as his car was not in the driveway. The garage had always been reserved for Ama, though there was a second garage for Robert's classic convertible, a 1929 Ford Model A that he kept from his father's days. Daniel had great memories of that car—going down the hill with his siblings to buy ice cream on the weekends, or fighting about who got to sit in the rumble seat in the back.

He rang the doorbell and soon heard footsteps approaching. He wasn't going to guess. . . .

The door opened, and there stood his dad. Neither man could speak. They hugged and cried like babies, but within a minute or two, they sat down. Robert wanted to ask Daniel a million questions, but he was paralyzed. All he could do was grab Daniel's shoulders, stroke his hair, and sob a bit more.

Daniel was very emotional, but he took control of his feelings and said, "Well, I'm here now."

"Darn it, your mom is always right," said Robert.

It was true that Ama had been very adamant that her son was not dead. Despite a few weak moments, she had kept saying to her husband, "Never give up on Robert. Never. He's alive; he's just not able to talk to us. Besides, Francesca said that he left of his own free will."

Daniel wanted so many questions answered, but first he had to know where his mother was.

"She takes my car now," said Robert. "I don't mind. She'll be here soon."

Daniel looked at the window, where San Francisco's airport was clearly visible, turned back to his dad, and said, "I have to ask some serious questions. I need to know the answers. It's killing me." He omitted the fact that he had three tiny memristors tucked between his skull and his scalp, but he began asking questions in a desperate attempt to understand his visions and the foreign languages he had begun to understand.

Robert jogged his memory to answer what he could. He did recall that Oakley was derived from Ballout—he had explained that to the kids at least once or twice, apparently when Daniel was too young to remember. According to Robert, before cutting a renegade baby oak tree that had sprung up at the back of the house, he once joked that his dad (Daniel's grandfather) would not have approved; oak was a sacred tree to the family, and it showed right on the coat of arm at the entrance to the house.

Daniel switched subjects and suddenly asked if his brother and sister were coming. They lived very close by, and he hoped they could be nudged to stop by for some reason. Daniel made it clear to his dad that he was an Indian national by the name of Adam Akamu. Robert was quick to reply, "I don't give a damn. You are alive and you are my son, and the rest is semantics."

It didn't take long for Ama to show up. She screamed, "I knew it, I knew it!" Daniel asked her to call him Adam.

"That's a silly joke," his mother remarked.

Robert asked Ama to listen to Daniel, who continued asking questions about his visions.

"So, Dad, tell me what you know about Topeka, Kansas. Did any of our family live there in the past?"

"Yes, I recall my grandfather talking about a cousin his dad had over there. I think he operated a general store."

"Was he in some kind of trouble?"

"Well, there's a story that he was robbed once when your own grandpa was visiting him from Mexico. Apparently he killed one of the colored assailants—in the old days they used that term for African Americans—but then he was shot in the face, in his left cheek, and he carried the mark until his death in the late 1950s or 60s."

"Okay. So far, so good, Dad."

"Are you looking up the family's history?"

"You might say that, Dad."

"By the way, he became a hero in that town. In those days justice was swift. They called him stormin' Herman; I recall that very well."

"And what about your own great-grandpa?"

"Well, he became fairly wealthy in Mexico, but his other son wasted all his money."

"What's going on with all these questions?" Ama asked.

"Well, Mom, now it's your turn. Did anyone from your family go to La Paz, Bolivia?"

"Yes, as a matter of fact. I think one of your . . . oh, great-grandfathers . . . they used to say how young he was when he died. He was alone, poor fellow. They found him days later. Your grandma would cry when she talked about him. Now, why do you ask?"

"It's nothing, Mom, but that's interesting. How young was he?"

"Oh, late thirties would be my guess, or even late twenties. He had his family first—you know, they married young in those days. Now, you need to tell us what's up with these questions."

"Well, it's beginning to make sense. I feel so much better. I've been having these dreams, and I confirmed every one of them. Dad, back to you: some of the dreams from when you were growing up are not very flattering. I won't ask you about those now, but I will ask if you were ever camping and had mountain lions come your way."

"Oh, son, yes. It was in Big Sur. I was with . . . um . . . *someone* in the tent, and I heard this roar. I looked up to see a large bobcat or a mountain lion crossing a broken tree over a creek—like a bridge, you know. We were on the opposite side of the creek, facing the cat. I was brave enough to grab some rocks and throw them at the beast, and it turned and ran. I did not sleep at all that night. We packed and left in the morning."

Ama remarked, "I'm glad you stayed up, honey. Who were you with?"

Daniel warned, "Mom, if you're going to be like that, I will stop."

Robert mused, "I have to tell you, Daniel, maybe you're having reincarnation episodes or something like that. You know, our family, prior to your and my generations, came from a religion called Druze, and they believed in reincarnation."

"Wow, Dad, that's interesting. You did mention it to us. Didn't you say that no one is allowed to leave the religion? I mean, once you're a Druze you're stuck, or something like that?"

"Yes. They won't kill you, but they will never consider you gone. Your Grandpa told me that our forefathers and foremothers had signed a pact called "Mithak", a contract that binds their descendants as well. Women signed, pretty advanced a 1000 years ago don't you think? He told me something else; the "Rule of Sevens" on how a Druze ought to raise kids; I suppose it works for none Druze as well.

"Nice, the West allowed women to vote just little over 100 years ago, what is the Rule of Sevens, do you remember?"

"From what I recall, a child's life is split in three time frames; from birth until the child reaches seven years old, parents ought to show love, care and affection with minimal discipline. From seven to fourteen you add discipline, teaching them how to read and write and finding academic strength or not I suppose. Beyond fourteen, parents should cut down on showing emotion, they need to add guidance to the subject matter the kid is enjoying until he or she becomes twenty one. That is when the child had reached complete independence and guidance is offered on demand, they're on their own by then. By the way it applies to both sexes and they don't need to know much about religion except for the 10 commandments until they reach forty, a nice long break don't you think?"

"So we are Druze, then."

"If you want, you can be—I don't have a problem with it. They're not bad people. Look them up and read for yourself."

"I have, Dad, in the past, just for my general education, but now I'm going to do a lot more."

Robert asked Daniel to look at one of the paintings hanging on the wall. Titled *Life,* it had been painted by Daniel's grandfather, Robert Sr. Daniel had never paid attention to its details or its meaning, even though it had not been moved from the same spot for over twenty years. It showed an old man standing on a rock and looking down at a canyon, where a river had been carving its way through the valley for thousands, if not millions, of years.

Robert said, "I recall my father talking about this scenery and explaining how life is like a river: rain collected in Earth's belly, going through the valley, taking sediments with it to the sea, creating these lines on the cliff, then coming back for more in the next season after evaporating. He would say that life, in flesh and blood, is only part of the grand cycle, and sediments are but experiences repeated and collected into life's large trash bin, sending the water along to the sea to go back for more… he would say often the "Universal Mind" sorry son, I don't know what he meant"

Daniel studied the painting further, and for the first time it meant a lot to him. Robert Sr. had painted with oil and without any formal education or training, but he had managed to produce some lovely art. A different painting had a couple wearing eighteenth-century clothes, and written on the back was *My Other Parents.* Yet another painting showed Robert's real father and mother, Daniel's grandparents. Could it be that Robert Sr. had a mild nirvana triangle at work? Was it possible to acquire one or to be born with one naturally? Something unusual had been going on with his grandfather, but unfortunately he was not there to answer.

Life

My Other Parents

Daniel missed his room downstairs, and he was happy to be back. It brought back memories of his breaks from Stanford — the calls, the studies, and so on. It was a productive room. He managed to reach his friend Maya in Honolulu and asked about Adam Akamu, and he learned that Adam had passed away the previous week in his hospital bed. Daniel was sad that he couldn't help in any way, and he promised to reach out to Adam's siblings and parents one day.

Francesca, on her end, had a sixth sense at work. She stopped by the Oakleys' house to see his parents while Daniel was downstairs. His parents were delighted to see her and assumed that Daniel had gotten hold of her.

Ama said, "Oh, I didn't think it would take very long for you to come."

"I just want to say hi."

"Well, go downstairs and say hi as much as you want."

"What's going on?"

"Didn't he call you? Daniel is downstairs!"

"Porco dio!" Francesca ran downstairs. She caught Daniel carrying one of his great-grandfather's paintings and looking at it very close, as if he were a museum forgery inspector.

It was a momentous reunion. Francesca cried and laughed, while Daniel became very emotional—though he controlled himself and avoided the embarrassment of shedding tears. The reunited couple came up with a game plan: They would not go out in public in the United States, and he would not visit Francesca's Danville home. For the time being, Daniel would still be Dr. Adam Akamu, a citizen of India. A plan that would work for the time being, but it would be tested in the near future.

Daniel told Francesca about his dreams and his nirvana triangle. The news amazed her, but mostly she was thrilled to see him alive and next to her. She told him that Dr. Wu had been arrested after passing on the Titan patent to Marco at Respi. Dr. Wu was later discharged, having been given a lighter sentence, because the Italian government had intervened on behalf of Respi and proved that the company was a trusted partner and had no malicious intent toward the United States. In fact, pointed out the Italians, the opposite was true: Respi was helping to expand Livermore's work. It was a good excuse for the Americans to have Italy on their side in the frantic race to create human titans. Respi truly wanted to help, and Dr. Wu had wanted to speed up their research and development without the usual red tape.

"It's too little too late," Daniel remarked. He was now preoccupied with explaining his visions. He felt better that his dreams had been vindicated, but he still wanted to create a time line of family events. He confirmed his mother's story about the La Paz ancestor with an old letter that his mother produced. But then he reasoned that if his great-grandfather had died alone, and having had kids prior to his death, how could this deathbed "memory", vivid with details, have been passed on to Daniel after the poor man had gone to the afterlife? He couldn't possibly have passed along this memory in a genetic, physical sense, could he?

It was a conundrum, but Daniel accepted Dr. Goyal's assertion that people's genes were embedded with layers of memory. Daniel himself was full proof. But how could this particular La Paz memory have traveled after death and passed on to him? Dr. Goyal had difficulty explaining how certain talents, such as music, sculpture, or painting, had come alive to a small portion of his patients. These talents had shown up at a late life stage and in raw form, so he knew they differed from so-called memory expansion; it was more that that. Talent was not evident in subjects before they had a chance to "upload" their Titans. Could it be a supernatural or scientific phenomenon not yet understood? Would Daniel know how to interpret this question?

God's particles

While the entire world was busy with heroes, apostles, the nirvana triangle, and so on, people were glued to the news as they waited for an impending conflict after each time the superpowers met. No one was paying attention to Higgs boson particles, known as God's particles.

Predicted by Peter Higgs in 1964 and confirmed in 2012, Higgs bosons confirmed the laws of quantum physics and nuclear science. They also confirmed that scientists were on the right track about the laws of creation. However, the question of *why* this boson field existed had remained unexplained. Higgs bosons would be dubbed God's particles because they were present everywhere; they constituted the element of mass in atoms. Scientists called them boson field matter because every atom gained mass by passing through this invisible field. Scientists struggling to explain the theory likened Higgs particles to a popular celebrity; the greater the celebrity, the more people gathered around to see him — and thus slowed him down. Therefore, a passing "celebrity" particle would encounter the masses — the Higgs bosons — which would get in its way and slow it down, thus imparting it mass. However, a particle such as a photon of light, which has no mass, is of no interest to the boson field and passes through easily.

Scientists came to believe that black holes, or dark matter, were packed with boson. Thus, Higgs bosons were one of the main ingredients of Earth's primordial soup — hence, God's particles. Daniel wondered if this field or fields have inherent intelligence — a marker or a signature to every living soul, animal and plant alike. What if humans had been selected to evolve such a complex brain or "Mind", attracting bosons that were particular to each individual's magnetic field? And what if, upon the person's death, they roamed freely until a similar living person bearing similar genetic markers attracted these particles' attention and permeated that person's conscience through his 'Mind', having uploaded their mass (memory) on atom particles they recognized as "celebrity" and enabling perpetual "Mind" continuity through many generations?. And what if this process was at work everywhere? Accountable for dreams and visions spoken about and responsible for the major religions on Earth. What if boson particles are attracted to matching "celebrities" regardless of the genetic similarities? and thus imparted on strangers at birth, or later in life. Could these wandering particles be in string formation? Dispersed upon person's death like tributaries carried by wind or earth's magnetic field join Boson Rivers that shape the 'Universal Mind'?

Daniel was onto something big. . . .

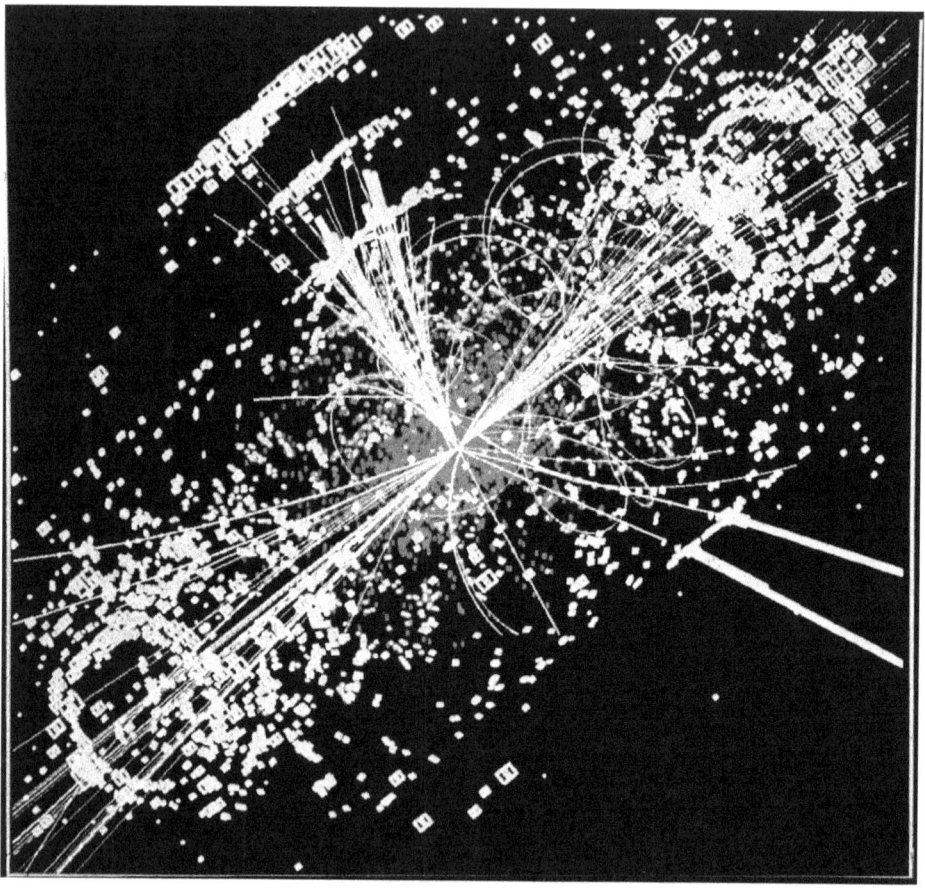

Higgs bosons briefly visible at the Large Hadron Collider in Switzerland

Crucial Background to the story;

The Druze are a relatively small Near Eastern religious sect that began during the rein of Al-Hakim Caliphate in Egypt in the year 1019 A.D. Characterized by an eclectic system of doctrines and by a cohesion and loyalty amongst their members. They became politically significant in the Levant thus enabling them to maintain through more than a thousand years of turbulent history their close knit identity and distinctive faith. Although preachers had set out of Cairo, the only communities that seemed to have embraced this new "Dawa" (call) where tribes inhabiting the rugged mountains of the Levant in today's Lebanon. They numbered more than 250,000 in the late 20th century and lived mostly in Lebanon, with smaller communities in Israel and Syria. Although supposedly warriors in nature, they had the "surprisingly civilized disposition and organization of the European" (La Martine ,1834) or "remnant of a French colony from the Crusades' Conte de Dreux" (Puget de Saint Pierre 1763) which he was mistaken. Lord Kitchener had set them apart as "the only tribes that are able to govern themselves" during WWI.

The Druze call themselves muahhidūn (monotheists) and the conception of the deity is declared by them to be one of strict and uncompromising unity. The main Druze doctrine states that God is both transcendent and immanent, in which he is above all attributes but at the same time he is present.

In their desire to maintain a rigid confession of unity, they stripped from God all attributes which may lead to polytheism (belief of multiple deities). In God, there are no attributes distinct from his essence. He is wise, mighty, and just, not by wisdom, might and justice, but by his own essence. God is "the whole of existence, the good and the bad" rather than "above existence" or on his throne, which would make him "limited." There is neither "how," "when," nor "where" about him; he is incomprehensible.

The Druze believe in the concept of Tajalli (Theophany), which is often confused with the concept of incarnation which is not part of their belief. Tajalli refers to the light and the understanding of God's creation mystery, experienced by certain mystics who have reached a high level of purity in their spiritual journey. Thus, God is perceived as the "Lahut" (Divine) who manifests this light in the temporal physical "stations" called "Maqam", which becomes a place of worship when that mystic dies. He or she would be known amongst the Druze to have a "Nasut" (purest soul) and prayers to the Divine (Lahut) would be conducted in his honor and on his or her burial grounds.

Reincarnation is another central part of their belief; a person's soul will continue to pass through successive periods of reincarnation, born into another human life, until it reaches the purity sought by the Divine in a union with "Moullaya Elakel" (Universal mind) and the individual's "Nasut" to reveal true God's will and how the Universe came to being.

The Druze scripture consists of five sacred texts including the "Kitab ElHikma" (Epistles of Wisdom).

In a 2005 a study of the ASPM gene variants was conducted by Mekel-Bobrov a scientist in Israel, found that the Druze people of the region have among the highest rate of the newly evolved ASPM haplogroup D, at 52.2% occurrence of the approximately 6,000-year-old allele. While it is not yet known exactly what selective advantage is provided by this gene variant, the haplogroup D allele is thought to be positively selected in populations and to confer some substantial advantage that has caused its frequency to rapidly increase.

According to DNA testing, Druze are remarkable for the high frequency (35%) of males who carry the Y chromosomal Haplogroup L which is otherwise uncommon in the Mideast (Shen et al. 2004). This haplogroup originates from prehistoric South Asia and has spread east to India into southern Persia.

Cruciani in 2007 found E1b1b1a2 (E-V13) [one from Sub Clades of E1b1b1a1 (E-V12)] in high levels (>10% of the male population) in Turkish Cypriot and Druze lineages. Recent genetic clustering analyses of ethnic groups are consistent with the close ancestral relationship between the Druze and Cypriots, and also identified similarity to the general Syrian and Lebanese populations, as well as a variety of Jewish lineages (Ashkenazi, Sephardic, Iraqi, and Moroccan) (Behar et al 2010).

Also, a new study concluded that the Druze harbor a remarkable diversity of mitochondrial DNA lineages that appear to have separated from each other thousands of years ago. But instead of dispersing throughout the world after their separation, the full range of lineages can still be found within the Druze population residing in the mountainous region of the Levant.

Researchers in Rappaport School of Medicine noted that the Druze villages contained a striking range of high frequency and high diversity of the X Haplogroup, suggesting that this population provides a glimpse into the past genetic landscape of the Near East at a time when the X haplogroup was more prevalent, predating the Canaanites and the Phoenicians.

These findings are consistent with the Druze oral tradition that claims that the adherents of the faith came from diverse ancestral lineages stretching back tens of thousands of years, having their genetic cluster coincide closely with those of the Samaritans and is very close to the genetic clusters of Ashkenazim, Sephardim, and Jews from the Caucasus.

The Druze symbol; Each color pertains to a metaphysical power called "Haad", literally meaning a limit, as in the limits that separate humans from animals, or the powers that makes the animal body human. Each Haad is color coded in the following manner: green for Agl "the Universal Mind/Nousse", red for Nafs "the Universal Soul/Anima mundi",yellow for Kalima "the Word/Loghos", blue for Sabiq "the Potentiality/ Cause/ Precedent", and white for Tali "the Future/Effect/ Immanence" . The mind generates qualia and gives consciousness. The soul embodies the mind and is responsible for transmigration and the character of oneself. The word which is the atom of language communicates qualia between humans and represents the platonic forms in the sensible world. The Sabiq and Tali are the ability to perceive and learn from the past and plan for the future and predict it.

For more please visit the American Druze Society at www.Druze.com

U.S Social security records;

HERMAN BALLOUT was born February 5, 1882, received Social Security Number 512-40-3591 (indicating Kansas), and died in February 1966. Wife to Beverly Ashcroft, father to Herman Badorct 1917 Rusk, Texas.

Husband	Wife
AMEEN, HERMAN	AMEEN, BEVERLY A.

Yosef Ballout (Jose Balut) 1883–1952 (Mexico City)

Hosein Chahine 1905- 1939 (Lapaz, Blovia)

****

Based on extensive DNA research and the newly discovered sequencing of RNA (ribonucleic acid) in populations, we now know that the Egyptians have been mixing with the rest of their neighbors since prior to the pharaohs and up to very recent times. Some even have direct lineage to people from France and Germany, probably due to the so-called Children's Crusade. The long-standing story was that Jesus went to Europe and simultaneously visited two boys: Nicholas, from the Rhineland, and Stephen, from the small French town of Saint-Denis. Jesus' common message was that there could no longer be infidels; everyone would convert, as long as they could hear the name of Christ the Lord. Hordes of children and adults followed Nicholas and Stephen as the news spread that they could perform miracles. In the summer of 1212 AD, the assembled crowd began marching to Jerusalem. Some took the boat from Genoa, only to be sold as slaves on the other side of the water. We are told that of the rest, none reached the Holy Land, and the divine message that Muslim infidels were ready to be converted to Christianity proved false. Damietta, on the northern tip of Egypt, received unwelcomed visitors again in 1221 AD. The participants of the fifth crusade, organized by Pope Honorius, got trapped in an unusual storm before trying to head for Acre. They had lost their battle with the Saracens, and while some managed to board the retreating ships, most stayed and converted to Islam, thus saving their lives by the order of Sultan al-Hakim. Most Egyptians today, especially those living around the ancient ruins, carry the same genetic imprints as the pharaohs who ruled thousands of years ago, and their DNA cocktails have similar levels of variation.

******

Café Barron had been around for sixty-five years. Several times it had changed owners, the last one being a gentleman by the name of Givo, who had taken over about a year ago. Robert Oakley, Daniel's dad, had worked with a renowned architect named Ahmad Mohazab on various architectural projects in food establishments, who was famous for designing the Citizens Building in downtown San Francisco, a 111-story tower shaped like an Arthurian sword. The building was owned by the Australian company IRG (Ian Rank Group), a wealthy mining business that had gained a foothold in the United States. They were famous for their uncanny ability to protect common people and companies from litigation. The company's famous ads on RadGio had created hype with slogans such as "IRG will see you in court, not me" and "IRG will make you think thrice—I, R, and G. Get it?" Other silly colloquial phrases have made the group famous. They lived up to their reputation by hiring young, gifted attorneys known for their tenacity and competence and by making sure the company showed them off for the world to see at every opportunity. Some of their famous cases involved celebrities such as actor Jeff Baldock and renowned pianist Serena Pucci, who were defended without pay if they would appear and praise IRG on RadGio. It worked so well that a great demand to enroll in law schools worldwide was attributed to the company's success, which in turn was attributed to the fact that its leaders were not ashamed to advertise and promote their lawyers. History had taught that having the right advice—and, better yet, the right defense, especially when one's case was weak and seemed hopeless—could make or break a case. IRG recognized this fact and would go to the rescue, step in, and win the day. Recently there had been a proliferation of IRG jokes, reminiscent of old Polish or Irish jokes of the previous century.

*****

In vivo experiments, or studies done on live animals, were widespread among medical faculties worldwide. The number of vertebrates used for testing, ranging from zebra fish to primates, was close to 150 million annually in 2031. Most animals were euthanized after being used in an experiment. The great demand had created a lucrative market for these animals. Companies procured their stock from a variety of sources; most animals were purpose bred, while others were caught in the wild or supplied by dealers who obtained them from auctions. Most softhearted organizations had understood the need for experimentation and thus had focused their efforts primarily on ensuring that the animals were treated humanely and all lab procedures were pain-free. There was a surprisingly large demand from the military industry for the use of animals in weapons and toxicology testing. Most genetic and biomedical studies were conducted inside universities and pharmaceutical companies, while behavioral and developmental studies were done mostly in medical schools. Some commercial facilities provided customized order studies, or COSs, for a particular field, such as developmental biology, as well as biomedical research, xenotransplantation, drug testing, and cosmetics testing.

Supporters of the use of animals in experiments, such as the Royal Society, argued that virtually every medical achievement in the twentieth and twenty-first centuries relied on the use of animals in some way. The Institute for Laboratory Animal Research of the U.S. National Academy of Sciences contended that because even the most sophisticated computers were unable to model interactions among molecules, cells, tissues, organs, organisms, and the environment, animal research was necessary in many areas. Some groups and animal-welfare organizations, such as PETA and BUAV, remained adamantly opposed to in vivo testing even after the Supreme Court ruling. They questioned the ethical and practical legitimacy of testing and killing lab animals by arguing that animal testing was cruel, scientifically unsound, and poorly regulated. They also contended that animal models were misleading obstacles to medical progress because they could not reliably help scientists predict effects in humans, that some of the tests were outdated, and that the costs outweighed the benefits.

Ultimately, they said, animals had an intrinsic and ordained right not to be used for experimentation.

******

The U.S. military had been on the forefront of medical research for decades. Conflicts in the previous century, including the Vietnam War and the wars in the Middle East, had spurred discoveries that prevented malaria and typhoid. Skin grafting in humans had been introduced during the Korean War and subsequently had been perfected, showing best results during the treatment of burn victims in the 2014 Saudi oil disaster at the Aramco compound. Military doctors had set particularly high standards and had improved triage care protocol. The old triage system had been based on the division of patients into three main categories: those who would not survive, even with treatment; those who would survive without treatment; and those whose survival depended on treatment. These new military doctors took greater risks by allocating medical resources to the first group and improving survival rates that would have been impossible just a few years earlier. The concept of triage had originated in the Napoleonic Wars, with the idea that treatment of patients who had a chance to live should not be delayed by useless or unnecessary treatment of patients who had little or no hope of living.

Among the military's newest innovations was BCX Bone Cement, an injectable compound for trauma victims who would have been left to die after a dose of morphine according to the old triage system. The idea had been copied worldwide. This new compound not only helped repair bones, but also could be used on the human skull to protect the brain in an emergency and, amazingly, to spur its growth. Thanks to bone cement, amputations were at a record low throughout the world.

Dr. Wu's career had put him in touch with the highest ranks of the military. In his position as head of the regenerative medicine department, he investigated risky measures that would prevent lifelong brain damage from war injuries. His department employed the world's best research scientists.

******

Part of President Tom Lieberman's speech for the Disabled Veterans at the White house had been to thank the MHD office for its creative work, for the support it had lent to inventors in the medical field, and for the "mighty American spirit of innovation that has and will change the world, time and again." Although the president was a Democrat, he ran on a fiscally conservative platform while sticking to the middle on social issues. He likened himself to John F. Kennedy. President Lieberman was very popular; he was relatively young, in his mid fifties, and had the backing of both houses of Congress. He had campaigned against Nick Dante, who had used Ronald Reagan as a benchmark for his campaign, giving rise to silly jokes such as "Grandparents' election" and "Young need not apply."

*****

The Vermeil Room had a unique history. The last time this large hall had been used was on July 17, for a private reception of the Euro Mediterranean Union (EMU) ambassadors, who had agreed to engage in a formal union with the European Union and to have rotating presidents from all member countries. Although the agreement had not been ratified by every country, it had laid the foundation for regulating immigration, the most pressing issue of the day. The EMU had been created in 1995 for the purpose of "turning the Mediterranean basin into an area of dialogue, exchange and cooperation guaranteeing peace, stability and prosperity," as written in its charter. It had been reinvigorated in

2008 with a treaty in Barcelona, where French president Nicolas Sarkozy had claimed the organization would "enhance multilateral relations, increase co-ownership of the process, set governance on the basis of equal footing and translate it into concrete projects, more visible to citizens. Now is the time to inject a new and continuing momentum into the Barcelona Process. More engagement and new catalysts are now needed to translate the objectives of the Barcelona Declaration into tangible results." The reception had included ambassadors from the European Union, as well as those from Mediterranean countries like Algeria, Albania, Cyprus, Egypt, Israel, Jordan, Lebanon, Malta, Montenegro, Morocco, Syria, Tunisia, and Turkey.

The Vermeil Room, although large, was the humblest in the White House. Originally it had been a staff workroom used for storing dried food and kitchenware and, in the 1880s, for polishing silver. It had been renovated in 1902, and during Theodore Roosevelt's administration it had been turned into a public room. It had remained opened to the public ever since, with various degrees of personal touch on furnishing from subsequent administrations, usually under the direction of First Ladies.

*****

Worldwide there were more than 50,000 NGOs, most of which were sponsored by the UN. The acronym NGO had been created along with the UN in 1945. These specialized non state agencies were awarded observer status when there was an international or domestic conflict that necessitated a UN Security Council meeting or assembly. In later times the term began to be used more widely until, according to the UN, any private organization that was independent of government control could be termed an NGO, provided it was nonprofit, noncriminal, and not simply an opposition political party. The organization also had to be validated as a voluntary citizens' group. The UN charter called for an

NGOs to be "... organized on a local, national or international level. Task-oriented and driven by people with a common interest, to perform a variety of services and humanitarian functions, bringing citizen concerns to light, through provision of information and organized around specific issues, such as human rights, environment and health. NGOs should provide analysis and expertise, serve as early warning mechanisms and help monitor and implement international agreements. Their relationship with offices and agencies of the United Nations system is streamlined and codependent on their goals, their venue and the mandate of the particular institution(s)."

****

Daniel's Great Grandparents